CW00863821

COME BACK TO ME

RONA JAMESON

To
Mum
Lots of Love
Rona Jameson
:)

Copyright © 2018 by Rona Jameson
All rights reserved.

No part of this book may be reproduced in any form or
by any electronic or mechanical means, including
information storage and retrieval systems, without
written permission from the author, except for the use
of brief quotations in a book review.

SYNOPSIS

Come Back to Me

When Esmé Rogers meets Luke Carlisle in 1987, she never expected to end up on board the Titanic for its maiden voyage from Southampton to New York in 1912. But what started with confusion and questions turns into the greatest love of her life.

As the date of the ill-fated sinking of the ocean liner approaches, Esmé questions whether or not she should try and change history. However, one question keeps coming back to haunt her: Does she survive?

With frigid waters and a predestined collision on the horizon, can she change the fate of those she loves?

To my family

CHAPTER 1

1987

Esmé Rogers flinched at the throb behind her temples. The pain had gained momentum and, with how sensitive she'd become, the sound of people murmuring and talking, along with loud laughter, silverware clinking, and even a dish breaking was making it worse. She wasn't sure how much more she could handle. Her fiancé, Jake, knew she was suffering, but he insisted on staying the course. The business dinner could see him as the new partner at the law firm where he currently spent all his time.

New York had changed her fiancé and she no longer felt like she was part of a couple. His long hours at the firm had put a distance between them, to the point she didn't really know him anymore.

She'd thought about leaving him. Maybe go back home. Then Jake would do something romantic, and she'd stay, even though she'd end up just as unhappy as before.

Esmé rubbed her temples again as she looked around the dimly lit room. Jars of decorative oils, dried pastas and hot peppers dotted the shelves around the small, family-run Italian restaurant. Waitresses rushed by in aprons with pens and pads sticking out of their pockets, and one guy nearly lost a tray of steaming food over two customers. He laughed it off while he quietly heaved a sigh of relief.

Her gaze slowly moved on and landed on an elderly man in a wheelchair who was seemingly staring back from under his lowered lids. He looked to have been a strong man once, but he'd lost his build and height with age. The more she stared, the more she thought he looked familiar. Maybe they'd met before?

She shook her head, which sent pain

from her neck to her temples, reminding her of the headache she'd been nursing.

Not wanting to join in with Jake and his guests, Esmé glanced back at the elderly man, and saw he'd whispered something to his companion—a granddaughter maybe, or even a great granddaughter? She was young, and looked around the same age as Esmé—twenty-five. Her thick blonde hair hung in long, graceful curls over her shoulders. She was petite and flowerlike.

The woman glanced over, holding Esmé's confused gaze while her companion continued to talk to her. Esmé sensed urgency in the man as he urged the young woman in her direction.

"Honey, Bill just asked you a question," Jake nudged her side. She ignored him and waited, knowing she was the final destination of the young woman.

Jake tried to snare her attention for a moment, until he gave up and mumbled something to his guests.

The young woman tugged anxiously on her slim fingers as she approached, her teeth worrying away at her bottom lip. She came to a stop directly in front of Esmé.

She inhaled deeply. "I know this is an unusual request." She glanced at her companion and then back to Esmé. "I'm Sienna Taylor, and I was wondering if you'd mind coming to meet Luke. I'm his caregiver. He's been agitated all day really. Now more than ever, saying he knew you a long time ago."

Sienna glanced over her shoulder again. When she focused on Esmé, tears sparkled in her eyes. She begged, "Please? I know he's imagining you." She softly laughed. "I mean you can't be much older than me, except to hear him talk, it's as though he knew you when he was our age." Taking her hand briefly, Sienna added, "In his own mind, he believes what he's saying, and, the thing is, I need him to calm down. He's a hundred and two, and...well, his health is failing." She twisted her fingers together. "I know he's done well to get to such an age, and I've grown to love him." She gave Esmé a watery smile.

As Esmé listened, her curiosity was piqued. What made this all the more intriguing was the fact that when she'd first set eyes on the man, he'd felt familiar.

She had a good memory for faces and his wasn't one that came to mind, but something told her she knew him.

Suddenly realizing she'd been sat staring, Esmé got to her feet and, as though in a trance, she walked beside Sienna toward the elderly man. "Can I ask you his name?"

"Luke Carlisle."

Luke Carlisle...How do I know you?

When she reached his side, Esmé pulled a chair close. Perched on the edge, she forced herself to lift her gaze to his face. His eyes were cornflower blue and glittered with an unknown emotion.

Luke reached out toward her with hands that trembled, so Esmé quickly covered his with her own. That's when she realized he was clutching something in his hand that he tried to pass her.

She took hold of what turned out to be an aged gold locket on a slim chain. Sienna gasped behind her, causing Esmé to sharply turn her head to look at the other woman, questions in her gaze.

"Luke's son, William, once told me that Luke wears a locket around his neck, and has done since he survived the sinking of the Titanic in 1912. William thought it had once belonged to a woman his father had met on board the ship. Luke would always get a faraway look on his face when I asked him about it." Sienna stared at the locket in Esmé's hand. "This is the first time I've seen it from around his neck," she whispered, looking at Luke in shocked surprise.

Esmé frowned, staring at the antique locket, covered with an intricate engraving of orange blossom flowers and swirling scrolls. She wondered why Luke had passed it to her if it obviously meant so much to him.

Old hands closed over hers and sealed her palm around the locket. "I don't know how," he whispered, "but I promised I would find you." Luke swallowed and started coughing. Sienna helped him take a sip of water and the coughing soon settled.

"I don't understand." Esmé shuffled closer. "How do I know you?"

"You actually know Luke?" Sienna asked,

kneeling on the floor beside his chair, her gaze on Esmé.

"I honestly don't remember," Esmé licked her dry lips, "but, everything about him teases at a memory."

Luke smiled softly and nodded his head. "You need to come back to me."

"What? Luke?"

He ignored Sienna and forced Esmé to meet his gaze. "Find me in the past... Please." As soon as the words left his mouth, his eyes drooped and he fell still and silent.

Panicked, Esmé quickly glanced at Sienna, who shook her head. "Don't worry. He's sleeping." Moving to the chair beside the one Esmé occupied, Sienna stared at the locket Esmé held in her hands.

"I don't understand any of this," Esmé admitted, looking at Sienna with pleading eyes. "Why? And what did he mean, 'find me in the past'? I need to talk to him again."

Sienna stared at her and then she nodded her head, as though she'd decided something. "Come to his home tomorrow morning." Sienna opened her purse and, after rooting around, handed a gold-embossed business card to Esmé. "He's more awake first thing in the morning, so hopefully he'll make more sense."

Inside, Esmé was shaking. "What time?"

"Anytime after seven-thirty."

Esmé nodded and slowly made her way back to where her angry fiancé waited.

CHAPTER 2

1987

Although Esmé hated the silence between Jake and herself, it was welcome. Her head continued to throb from her migraine. But it hadn't stopped spinning since her unexpected meeting with Luke Carlisle.

The elderly man had certainly been adamant that he knew Esmé. It completely baffled her. But there had been something familiar about him. She'd felt it in the restaurant. What had it been? His voice? His eyes had been clear and focused on her face —almost unnervingly so.

He was a puzzle Esmé needed to solve. She wouldn't be able to rest until she'd discovered more about Luke and how she was connected to him. She didn't doubt there was a connection. It was there, when he'd touched her hand. Luke had pleaded with his eyes, and she'd been disappointed with herself—she hadn't properly understood what he'd wanted from her. His words 'you need to come back to me' wouldn't leave her mind.

Her gaze turned to the beautiful locket in her hand and jumped when Jake stormed out of the bathroom, showered and ready for bed. He was tall, medium build with a head full of tawny-gold hair. Right now his square jaw was visibly tensed.

He sighed after closing his side of the closet with another thump. He turned to Esmé, his hazel eyes full of anger. "Would it hurt you to show your support for my career once in a while?" He moved over to the bed. "Instead of being indifferent," he hissed.

The large throw pillows landed on the floor as he yanked the covers down and crawled under them. "I know you hate the business dinners, but tonight was important," he continued to rant.

"I'm sorry Jake. My migraine got in the way and then the elderly man distracted me." Esmé frowned and rubbed at her brow. "He said he knows me but I don't see how. I don't remember him. However there's something about him..." She trailed off.

Collecting her nightgown from the armchair at the side of the bed, Esmé glanced at Jake. "I really am sorry." And she was. She'd let him down, regardless of their lives moving in different directions.

Slipping inside the bathroom, Esmé locked the door and, resting her hands on the vanity, stared at herself in the mirror. Her body was slender, with dark auburn hair falling to her waist. Her fiery, emerald green eyes glowed from her delicate face. Although she was tired and still in pain from the headache, her face shone with peach undertones.

Her gaze dropped once again to the chain and locket as her fingers caressed over the engraved design. With delicate fingers, she picked it up and slipped it over her head, around her neck. She tried to open the locket but it wouldn't budge. Maybe it had gotten stuck with age.

Too tired for anything other than sleep, Esmé quickly changed into her nightgown, the locket hanging between her breasts.

She glanced at the closed, bathroom door and prayed Jake was already asleep. She'd sensed his anger through the door. She knew he'd really wanted to rage at her —that it had taken a lot on his part to reign in his temper.

CHAPTER 3

1987

Esmé's stomach rolled as she stood on the stoop of the townhouse where Luke Carlisle lived with his caregiver. She rested the palm of her hand against the black front door, her head dipped while she mustered the courage to knock.

She needed an explanation for the locket hidden beneath her clothing.

The brass door knocker called to her, however, before she reached for it, the door swung open. Sienna stood there with red and watery downcast eyes. "I wasn't sure if you planned on knocking or not," Sienna said in response to Esmé's startled gasp.

Sienna backed up into the house, leaving Esmé with no choice except to follow, which she did, although tentatively.

The first thing Esmé noticed when she stepped inside the spacious entryway was the chandelier that dropped three floors. Her eyes followed the curved staircase to the ground floor and the dark hardwood flooring under her booted feet. As she followed Sienna upstairs, she took in the decor. The walls displayed artwork, but nothing modern.

The young woman from the night before had disappeared and the silent woman in front of her looked...*lost.*

At the top of the stairs, Esmé reached out and placed her hand on Sienna's arm. "What's happened since last night?"

Sienna turned slowly but she couldn't hide the tear slipping down her cheek. "I had to call the doctor... He doesn't have long left."

Shocked, Esmé snatched her hand back and clutched at her chest.

"Old age," Sienna added, offering a sad smile. "He's waiting for you."

Esmé followed her down a short hallway full of more antique paintings until they stopped outside a dark paneled door.

"I'll let you go in alone." Sienna backed away and without another word, disappeared the way they'd come, leaving Esmé to ponder her entrance.

Esmé's heart beat franticly in her chest and because her palms were sweaty, she had to wipe them on her jeans before she finally felt brave enough to enter.

When she did, she found Luke propped up in the middle of a large king-sized bed. The room was filled with dark furniture. A machine beeped at the side of the bed and another machine hissed with oxygen.

"You came," Luke said in a tired voice filled with hope.

Esmé moved closer. Unable to find a chair to sit on, she settled into the side of the bed when Luke patted it with his frail hand. Her gaze lifted to his face, and she asked him the question most on her mind. "Why are you familiar to me?"

He closed his eyes and concentrated on breathing for a few minutes. Just when

Esmé thought he'd fallen asleep, his lids opened and he said, "We met," he had a whimsical smile on his lips, "a very long time ago." Paused. "You were everything to me, and then you disappeared."

The confusion Esmé felt must have been clear on her face because Luke appeared sad. "You think I'm crazy. Just an old man with a wandering mind."

"No." Esmé dropped her purse to the floor and reached out for his hand. The minute they touched, she was overwhelmed with feelings. Her memory tried to reach for something...something to do with this man...but she couldn't grasp it before it was gone. "I believe you, but I don't know why? Or how?" She shook her head in wonder.

"I've spent a long time waiting for this moment, and now, I can finally rest in peace."

"But..." His words had sounded so final.

"Nothing makes sense to you right now. I know." Sadness seeped from him before he took a minute to catch his breath. "I know because, when you left me, I was bereft, out of my mind with heartache…and then, I knew."

"Knew what?" Esmé moved closer. She was so close, she could see every wrinkle on a face she knew but couldn't place. It was his eyes and the way he watched her.

"I knew I had to wait to see you again… to give you this." He lifted his other hand, which was too weak to go far so Esmé leaned over and took an old plated photograph from his hands.

It was much heavier than today's photographic print. It was brown in color with an image of a couple in eveningwear. She looked closely, and her surprise was evident as she mumbled words that made no sense, finally, she met Luke's damp eyes. "That… that can't be me. How is that possible? It has to be a relative?"

Her eyes focused on the picture again. This time she took note of the man in the photograph dressed in evening attire. His clothing was neat, and while she had no way of knowing, seemed expensive. They fit his tall, muscular frame well. Short dark hair was swept back from his face, looking tidy, except it was his eyes that held her attention —like now. He was handsome with a secret expression on his full lips. Even on the old photographic plate, his love for the woman on his arm was evident.

"I'm tired now," he mumbled.

She blinked at the man in the bed and felt her heart crack. She didn't understand what was happening or why she had so much emotion running through her. How could she? After all, she'd only met the man last night...she couldn't remember meeting him before that. Ten minutes later, Luke opened his eyes and stared straight at Esmé. "Will you lift my hand to your face? I want to touch you one final time."

Esmé caught her breath and tears hovered on her lashes when she moved his hand until his palm covered her cheek.

He brushed his thumb over her skin, his palm held steady. "Just as I remember."

When his arm started to tremble, she gently laid it back on the bed and kept her hand in his.

"I'm not going to wake up again," he whispered, squeezing her hand. Then he whispered the words that she was sure would haunt her for the rest of her life, "I never stopped loving you. It was only ever you. Come back to me, Esmé."

Luke Carlisle took his last breath.

CHAPTER 4

1987

"You need to snap out of this," Jake barked, anger dripping from every word. "Ever since that old man died two weeks ago, you've been acting like a ghost. You're here with me, but you're not, are you? You don't care whether or not I get the promotion. You don't care about anything!" He paced back and forth like a sentry—stiff in his rage.

Esmé only paid half attention to him while she counted the minutes until he would leave for work. She wanted to look into what Luke had given her.

The past couple of weeks had been a

COME BACK TO ME

blur for Esmé while she'd grieved from the loss of Luke. She'd felt his love for her and, although she hadn't understood it, her heart had broken in two when Luke had died while she'd held his hand. She hadn't been able to understand the melancholy that had taken hold of her...it refused to let go. It was as though she'd lost her parents all over again, which made her feel guilty. The way she felt at the loss of Luke was ten times stronger, and she couldn't understand why.

Ever since Luke had given her the picture of him and the woman who *had* to be a relative of hers, she'd been unable to concentrate on anything else. She needed answers because there was no way the image was of her. It was impossible. Except, Luke had believed it was her.

Sienna had been surprised to discover the photograph Luke had given her. Especially after she'd really looked at the woman on the image. At Luke's funeral, Sienna had asked Luke's Grandson, David, but he'd never seen the photograph before. So Esmé hoped that later in the day, when she paid a visit to Frederick Fitzwilliam, he'd have answers. The man owned an old photography store and was the fifth generation to run the place. She figured if anyone did, he'd know something about dating photographs.

"Dammit Esmé!"

Esmé jumped in surprise.

Jake glared at her profile before he slammed out of the door.

With a huge sigh of relief, Esmé fingered the locket around her neck, overwhelmed with sadness. Nothing had made sense to her from the moment she'd met Luke Carlisle. The man had been a total enigma.

Esmé checked the time, and decided Jake would have left the building, so she turned and quickly headed for the hall closet. She'd hidden everything she'd need for the day while Jake had been busy elsewhere. He'd been watching her like a hawk for weeks and she'd finally had enough.

She needed to end her engagement to Jake because she didn't think either of them wanted to go through with it anymore. She didn't love him, and she wasn't sure she ever had.

But her thoughts weren't for Jake—they were for Luke. Until she had answers, she didn't think she'd be able to carry on with her life whether or not she was still with Jake.

Sighing heavily, she left her apartment and climbed straight into the cab that the doorman had called for her. Esmé gave the driver the address and twenty minutes later she found herself outside of the photography store.

She glanced up at the chained sign to make sure she had the right place. She did.

The black awning looked well past it's used by date, and the windows needed a good scrub.

Her excitement about receiving answers began to dwindle as sadness settled into her shoulders. The neglected property didn't look like anyone had been inside for a long time, which meant dear *Frederick* wouldn't be around.

"Are you looking for me?"

She turned quickly, stumbling, and just managed to catch herself on a wrought iron lamppost.

The man quickly dashed over and grabbed her arm. "I'm so sorry. I didn't mean to startle you." He let go as quickly as he'd touched her and nodded at the closed store. "That's me. Frederick Fitzwilliam. I thought maybe you were a customer." He shrugged and stepped back, giving her space.

"Esmé Rogers." She wrapped an arm around her stomach and took a chance. "I have an old photograph that I'm trying to date. Maybe find where it was taken as well. It's a plate."

"Ah! Come with me." The man rubbed his hands together, full of excitement. "I haven't had a challenge in years." He fidgeted with his keys and after the fourth attempt, found the correct one.

Frederick was in his thirties, not very tall, with pale, receding, overlong hair, and a slight paunch. He certainly seemed friendly enough, but time would tell.

At least Sienna knew she was at the store in case Esmé didn't check in with her soon. No doubt the other woman would call her, desperate for information. Esmé hoped she'd have something to tell Sienna, as she followed the excited man into the store.

"Let me get some lights on." No sooner had the words left his mouth than the room was flooded with light. It was so bright— Thomas Edison would be happy to see such a display.

"I need light to be able to work. You'll get used to it." He dropped his satchel to the floor and urged her over to a rather old desk.

Esmé ran her fingers over the edge and, surprisingly, didn't find any dust. "Nice desk," she said to hide her embarrassment at being caught.

She cleared her throat and with a slight hesitation she didn't understand, removed the plate from the protective case she'd placed it in.

Sliding it onto the light box, Frederick gasped in delight. His eyes wide, he asked, "Where did you get this?"

"Someone left it to me. What can you tell me about it?"

"What?" He jumped from his chair and moved so close to the photograph, his nose almost touched it. "You have a remarkable resemblance to this woman," he muttered.

Her belly quivered with unease but Esmé hid her reaction behind a smile. "So I've been told." Clearing her throat, she added, "Other than the likeness I have for her, is there anything else you notice?"

"Hmm." He placed an eyeglass against his eye and stared at the photograph. She'd only ever seen jewelers use them. Seconds later it fell out. He dropped down heavily into the chair behind him. "That can't be right."

"What is it?" She leaned forward, eager to hear what he had to say.

"Let me look again." He picked up the eyeglass, his hands shaking, and his body tensed, as he took a long look at the photograph.

"You say someone left you this?" He looked at her full of curiosity.

She offered him a brief explanation. "The man who gave me this, died not more than five minutes later. He was over a hundred years old." She fought back tears.

"Please," she begged, "I need to know about this photograph."

"This photograph was taken on board the RMS Titanic. I can't tell you the exact date it was taken but the liner sailed her maiden voyage on April, 10th 1912. She hit the iceberg on April, 14th and sank to the bottom of the ocean a few hours later, on April, 15th. This photograph was taken between those dates." Esmé sat in stunned silence while Frederick grinned full of excitement. "It can't be seen with the naked eye, but with the eyeglass, I can just make out the writing on the door that they're standing beside." He pointed with a thick finger. "See…"

He passed the eyeglass to Esmé, who took it in her trembling hand while Frederick turned the photograph around. With butterflies in her stomach, she looked, and immediately saw what he had. RMS Titanic in gold letters.

Esmé sat back down with a thud, her heart racing. "That can't be." Even as she'd said those words, she knew the true date of the photograph was 1912. She should have known because Sienna had told her how Luke had been a survivor of the Titanic sinking.

But who was the woman in the photograph...she needed answers. She passed the eyeglass back and asked, "Can you look at the woman and tell me if there is any marking on her...neck?"

Frederick gave her an odd look, but took the eyeglass and buried his face in the photograph again. He frowned and met her gaze. "How did you know?"

She took a deep, shaky breath. Slowly, she pulled her silky scarf away from her neck. "I didn't, but I thought I would have answers. Although I do, I'm still as confused as ever... Is this the mark you see on the photograph?"

"Yes," he whispered, bewildered. "Now, I'm confused."

She held his gaze, and then jumped up with the sudden urge to leave. "I need to go," she gasped in panic. "Thank you for your help." Esmé quickly pocketed the photograph. "How much do I owe you?"

"You owe me nothing, but you can't

leave now," he begged, following her to the door. "I need to know more!"

"I'm really sorry." Esmé turned and ran from the store. She didn't stop running for three blocks until she couldn't catch a breath.

She gasped and moved slowly back and forth, forcing her breathing to become even. Only then did she step into a telephone booth.

Sienna answered on the first ring. "I've been waiting for your call."

Esmé didn't know what to tell Sienna. It wasn't like she could tell Sienna about the small beauty mark the woman had—the exact same mark on the right side of her own neck. Not over the telephone anyway. Her mind whirled around the possibilities and all the questions it raised.

"Esmé, are you still there?"

"April, 1912," she blurted out. "Sienna, the photograph was taken on board the RMS Titanic."

"But...oh! Could he tell you anything about the woman?"

Esmé let Sienna's question hang in the

air, not wanting to answer. Then she suddenly realized where she was, and what was across the street... New York Public Library. They'd have some way of looking up people, and they'd also have all the newspaper archives from 1912. Wouldn't they?

CHAPTER 5

1987

Esmé felt a nervous flutter in her belly as she entered the library. She hadn't visited since she'd arrived in New York. The bookstore close to her apartment building was a favorite of hers so she never made it down to the library.

As she glanced around looking for the reference section, she smiled when she noticed a group of children surrounding a large table to the left. They were busy listening to one of the librarians while their teacher kept a close eye on them. Esmé sometimes missed the simplicity of childhood.

Slowly moving to the long front desk

manned by the librarians and their assistants, Esmé waited her turn. The whir of a copy machine drew her gaze and once it had tossed out the last piece of paper, the loud tick of the clock grew annoying.

Her gaze wandered over the bookshelves lining the walls that marched across the floor in rows, curling around reading nooks and study areas.

A throat being cleared caught her attention. "Can I help you?" a middle aged librarian asked.

Esmé smiled. "Please can you tell me where I might find a list of survivors from the Titanic?"

The woman tsked in clear irritation. "Really? Why?"

"I just really need to see the list." Esmé felt like snapping at the woman.

Her jaw tightened. "It could take a while to find."

Esmé held her ground and just stared at the woman. Finally, the woman sighed in irritation. "Follow me then."

Esmé rolled her eyes but held her tongue. There was no rush to the woman at

COME BACK TO ME

all, whereas, Esmé felt filled with impatience.

The woman led her through rows and rows of thick dictionaries, encyclopedias, atlases and what appeared to be historical texts before she indicated for Esmé to sit in front of a microfilm machine.

"Give me a few minutes to find the relevant information." The woman stomped off, her feet thudding on the hardwood floor as she moved away, her temper obvious.

Hopefully she'll be back.

A loud sneeze made her jump, which was followed by a whispered, "Excuse me." Two more rapid sneezes, and Esmé chuckled silently.

Five minutes passed before the sour librarian returned. "This has the information on it. Do you know how to work the machine?" she asked, rudely stuffing a sheet of paper toward Esmé's chest.

"Yes." *No, but she'd figure it out.*

"Very well," she huffed.

Once the woman disappeared, Esmé breathed a sigh of relief and after five minutes, had the machine up and running.

She felt almost scared of what she would find, but she had to know if, by some unexplained reason, she'd been on the Titanic with Luke. Was she crazy for listening to him? She hoped not because he'd certainly believed what he had said.

The names of the first class passengers started to appear and Esmé's belly fluttered. When she saw Carlisle, Luke, her heart raced. Her hand working the machine froze.

Everyone had said Luke had been on the ship; seeing his name shouldn't be such a surprise. However, it was.

All the blood thrummed through Esmé's ears as she quickly found 'R'. There was no one by the name of Rogers on the list. Not as a first class passenger. Tears momentarily blinded her as she became overwhelmed with disappointment. As strange as it was, she'd hoped to find her name.

She quickly checked second and third class lists, but nothing. No Rogers. Nothing.

Her hands trembled as she placed the film back into the container. She grabbed a tissue from her purse, wiped her face, and quickly composed herself before she thanked the librarian and left.

Outside, on the steps of the library, she sank down. Her mind was spinning with thoughts of Luke. He had been so adamant about her finding him. The photograph he'd given her had been taken on board the ship and it was her. It had to be because the resemblance was remarkable. So why wasn't her name on a list?

It didn't make sense. In fact, nothing made sense to her anymore.

CHAPTER 6

1987

"Do you think I'm crazy?" Esmé asked. She'd finished telling Sienna about the photograph, including how the woman had a beauty mark in the same place as hers.

"If I hadn't seen Luke's reaction to you, then I would say yes. But, he was so adamant he knew you. He said he'd been waiting all these years for you. I don't understand it. But he believed you were...are...the woman in the photograph."

Esmé watched as Sienna worried at her bottom lip before moving over to the dining table in the old town house. Everywhere Esmé looked, the furniture was old, dark wood. It would have been expensive at one time. Sienna caressed the table with her small hand before she picked up a large, brown box that looked as old as the furniture. It was tied with a ribbon, the color of which looked to have faded over the years.

Sienna's eyes shifted to Esmé as she slowly made her way over to the couch and placed the box on top of the coffee table. "I found this at the back of Luke's closet." She took a seat directly opposite from Esmé, and continued, "It says *Esmé Rogers* on the name tag... I assume it's for you."

Esmé's eyes snapped up to Sienna, who seemed to hesitate, before she added, "The box and tag were covered in a thick layer of dust. They'd been there for years, I guess."

Dropping to her knees from the sofa, Esmé moved closer and hesitated before she fingered the tag. Her name had been written in a bold script with the words, "Wear this and find me in the past. Yours forever, Luke."

Color drained from Esmé's face as the blood rushed from her head. She felt lightheaded. Grabbing the coffee table in front of her, her mind spun with emotion.

"I wish I knew what was going on." Esmé breathed heavily and glanced up, finding Sienna just as shocked. "I searched the archives for Luke, and he was there on the passenger list, but...I wasn't."

She pushed herself to a standing position and on legs that trembled, Esmé slowly moved over to the oval window. She looked out into the back garden. She didn't notice the scenery outside, instead, she was lost in her own thoughts as she wrapped a hand around the locket. All she saw was the image of Luke before he'd died, and the photograph that had been preserved all these years.

She'd felt drawn to him like nothing before, and the more she discovered about Luke, the more she was starting to realize that, maybe, there was truth to his story...she just didn't understand how it was possible.

"Will you open the box?" Sienna asked from across the room. "I haven't touched it other than to bring it downstairs. I'm really curious, and maybe there are answers inside."

Esmé's stomach fluttered, more with nerves than excitement. With a tremble to her hand, she reached up and rubbed her temples, willing the throb to disappear while she stared at the mystery box.

It wouldn't open itself.

Reluctance in every step, Esmé moved to the box. She dropped to her knees, hesitating as she stared at the gift tag again. Finally, with care, she unwound the pink ribbon, folded it and placed it into the top of her purse. The gift tag followed. Swallowing hard, she closed her eyes and before she backed away, she quickly lifted the lid from the box.

At Sienna's gasp, Esmé's eyes snapped open and she looked into the box. The shock of discovery hit her full force and her bottom hit the floor. "It's the dress," she whispered, her voice breaking slightly. "The one in the photograph." She crawled back to the small table and gently laid a palm against the soft material. The black and white, slightly browned photographic plate hadn't done the dress justice. It was powder pink with deeper pink flowers, the material soft and old to the touch.

Taking hold of the dress by the shoulders, Esmé lifted it out of the box, unfolding it gradually, until the beauty of the dress could be seen. The dress cinched at the waist with a small broach, a matching one further down the dress, until the deep pink flowers became larger as the dress trailed to the floor.

Suddenly, Sienna started laughing, which snapped Esmé out of her trance. She glanced at the other woman and her eyes widened in surprise when Sienna held out a chemise with a ruffled neckline and drawers in white cotton. She placed them over the back of the sofa before she pulled out a corset in fine silk. "There's also a pair of matching silk shoes and stockings." Sienna leaned over, smoothing her fingers over the silk of the dress. "It's all beautiful."

"I need a drink." Esmé groaned. "What are you actually thinking?"

"Apart from the fact that I'm considering joining you for that drink, only I don't drink, I'm thinking something real is happening here. I thought he was crazy, but he wasn't, was he? From what I've been told, Luke hadn't gotten around under his own steam for years, which means all this had to have been planned before then."

Sienna sat down heavily, the corset draped over the box. "I don't know how it's possible for you to have been there with him in 1912. It has to be a relative of yours, right?"

A long silence followed. "Neither of us believe that." Esmé finally sighed.

"I want to believe because it's logical, but," Sienna dashed around the coffee table and, taking hold of Esmé's hands, continued, "what if you were there? What if, somehow, you went back in time?"

Esmé stared at Sienna, wanting to believe her. She couldn't fathom the possibility of time travel.

"Look," Sienna started, "I know I sound crazy, but, think about it... He knew *you*. He's had this box stored in his room for years. You only have to look at it all to realize the facts."

Esmé felt as pale as the white chemise.

"The box was gifted with my name, before I was born."

Sienna suddenly snapped. "Did you check on the surviving passenger list for an Esmé Carlisle? What if you both were married?"

Esmé blinked. "I never gave that a thought." She frowned. "I don't think so because the surnames were alphabetical, and there was only one Carlisle."

"Oh." Sienna fidgeted, trying to hide her disappointment.

Esmé wrapped an arm around her midriff and after moments of silence, cleared her throat. "What do you know about Luke?"

Sienna shrugged her shoulders. "Nothing much, really. I've only lived here to care for Luke for around two years. His son, William, has Alzheimer's. William's son, David, is hardly ever around. But I do know that Luke adopted William in 1912 after William's parents, Olive and Matthew, died. They were onboard the Titanic and never made it home. They'd left William in New York with his grandparents, so lucky for him, I guess."

"I don't know what to say." She cleared her throat, needing to leave and have her own space to think. "I need to head home and think about everything. I just can't process it all." She sighed. "I also need to be home before Jake gets there."

"Does Jake know you no longer wish to marry him? You could always move in here if you need somewhere to live. I'm sure William wouldn't mind." She shrugged. "I'm staying to help William because, before too long, his Alzheimer's will get worse."

Esmé offered a wry smile. "I haven't told Jake yet. My mind has been preoccupied." Esmé shrugged, getting everything back into the box.

"Will you be all right?" Sienna asked, worried.

"I will be." Esmé gathered her belongings together. "I'll see you tomorrow." Hefting the box under one arm, she quickly left before she changed her mind about leaving. She felt overpowered with raw emotion whenever she was in the house, and it frightened her. Something was happening and she felt that everything she'd learned was the truth. Something told her that no matter how farfetched it seemed she had been on the RMS Titanic with Luke.

CHAPTER 7

1987

Esmé was frustrated. The locket Luke had given to her refused to be opened. And it looked too fragile to be forced open; she'd been tempted to try with a knife.

Even glaring at the antique piece hadn't helped, although she didn't know what she'd expected. It currently sat on the coffee table in the apartment she shared with Jake, the bright sunlight shining on it.

The apartment she called home was modern with the newest of furniture. The opulent fireplace was her favorite feature and had sold her on the apartment in the first place. The entire apartment had been decorated around that fireplace, although, the floor-to-ceiling windows boasted a wonderful skyline view.

The artwork on the walls had been Jake's idea and she didn't care much for any of it. The throw rugs on the floor in front of the fireplace had been her idea and she loved them, and the bit of color they gave the apartment. If only material things made her happy.

Her eyes strayed back to the locket just as someone knocked on her door. She frowned, wondering whom it could be considering she lived in an apartment building with a concierge, and security. Requirements Jake had insisted on.

Peering through the peephole, she saw the doorman fidget in his grey uniform.

Curious, she tugged the door open, and to her surprise, realized he wasn't alone.

"The courier has a letter for you," he supplied.

"I have strict instructions to give it to you, and no one else, on this date. The lawyer was insistent it can't be delivered before or after," the courier admitted, holding out a letter. "You need to sign for it. I get a bonus when I provide proof you received it on this date. So please can you date your signature?" Thrusting a clipboard into her hands, the courier passed her a pen and she quickly signed and dated the delivery note.

When she glanced at her name on the envelope, she felt the color drain from her face. The writing was in the same bold script as the tag on Luke's box.

"Thank you," she mumbled and closed the door on them.

The doorman, Jim, would want to know about the letter. She knew he was a gossip and he'd want to know her reaction, but the letter was private.

Her legs quivered as she moved slowly into the living area and sat down on the sofa. Nervous fingers ran over the name on the envelope and trembled with shock.

Why would Luke send her a letter only to be delivered to her on a certain date? Was it to explain what was happening?

She felt sick to her stomach at the thought of the words he'd written. Scared to open the envelope, her need to know more about Luke ate at her.

Before she could change her mind, she tore into the envelope and pulled out a cream colored sheet of paper.

Tears hovered on her lashes when she looked at the signature on the bottom of the letter: Yours forever, Luke.

"Oh!" She clutched the letter to her chest while tears slowly trickled down her face. She didn't fully understand why she was reacting this way, but she desperately needed to put the pieces together—the pieces that would lead her to Luke Carlisle.

Perhaps the letter would shed some light on it.

With that thought, she inhaled deeply before slowly exhaling, and opened the letter fully.

1987

My dearest Esmé,

A long time ago you wrote me a letter, which I received after you left me. I eventually learned that what you told me was the truth. I don't know how or why you were given to me on the Titanic, but I fell in love with you completely in the short time we were together.

My life when you disappeared had no meaning. I couldn't step outside without hoping to find you amongst the crowds of people. Every time someone came calling to the house, I prayed it was you coming home to me. Of course, it never was, but I never gave up hoping that one day we would be reunited.

Not a day went by where I didn't look at the beautiful locket you left behind and cried over your loss. I missed you with every beat of my heart.

I truly believe we will be together again one day, which is why I need you to trust me and find me in the past.

On April 10th, 1912, we met on the promenade of the RMS Titanic, as it was untangled from its near miss with the New York at Southampton. I remember this day like it happened yesterday, and not years ago.

My heart jumped from my chest to yours at first sight and you've held it for all these years.

I wish I knew how everything worked but I, unfortunately, don't. All I know is I've done everything I can think of to bring you back to me.

The clothing I left you in my closet, which I know Sienna will have found by now, must be worn without ANY modern day clothes, as well as the locket. That's all I know.

If everything I've done turns out to not be enough for us to meet in 1912, and you become a figment of my imagination, know I have loved you with every breath I took.

If you are successful and get back to me, know that a love like ours will never die and will only flourish.

This letter might sound like an old man rambling, but I can assure you, for all my fragility, I am of sound mind.

I wish I could warn you about how you ended up back in 1987, but I'm hoping by not saying anything, it won't happen again. Selfish maybe, but after the lonely years I've lived, I want you by my side forever.

You see, until you find me in 1912, our destiny together hasn't properly been set. Everything can change.

Come back to me Esmé.

Yours forever,

Luke

CHAPTER 8

1987

Esmé's face was still damp from the tears she'd shed after reading the letter. Her heart ached for what he must have gone through, and, in turn, she felt wrecked. It surprised her to realize she wanted Luke's imaginings to be true. She wanted to go back to him. She wanted to experience the love Luke was convinced they had once shared.

As sad as it was to admit, Esmé had never had deep feelings for Jake. Even worse, she thought Jake was having an affair and the only thing that bothered her about it was the fact that he still acted as though they were a couple. They weren't. Not really. Jake knew it too.

It was late as she looked out across the dark New York night, but what she really looked at was the reflection of the demure gown hanging on the closet doors behind her.

She had so many questions, the main one being, how was she on the ship? She needed that one answered above anything else. Of course she wanted to know more about Luke, but it sounded to her as though everything started with the Titanic. Luke had certainly believed that.

Turning to face the closet, her eyes landed on the beautiful dress. She'd never seen anything like it before, and the temptation to try it on was eating away at her. Why not? The dress had been gifted to her so she had every excuse to play dress up.

So why was she so reluctant?

Luke's letter had been burning in her mind since she read it earlier that day. She wondered about the significance of wearing the locket while wearing the clothing he'd left for her. So far she'd been unsuccessful at opening the locket.

With a heavy sigh, she mumbled, "I'm

not reluctant!" With determination in her step, she quickly removed her clothes. Inhaling and slowly exhaling, she stepped into the all-in-one chemise and drawers, twirling in front of the mirror, which made her laugh at the sight before her.

It certainly made her heart lighter. It was fun wearing the old clothing. She'd think about everything else later but, for now, she had a dress to get into. Esmé ignored the corset because it looked like it would be torture.

With care, she gingerly stepped into the gown of finest silk, pulling it up her slender limbs, over her hips and eventually, she slipped her arms through the delicate cap sleeves. Once fastened, she slipped her feet into the silk stockings and then the shoes, not even surprised when everything fit perfectly. The white stockings felt odd on her legs since they only came to mid-thigh. As a rule, she hated anything other than slacks or jeans on her legs.

Slowly turning, Esmé was surprised to see a regal woman staring back at her. She was slender, medium height, and had eyes sparkling with emotion. Her bone structure was delicately carved, her mouth full. The rich auburn hair shone under the light of the room. She was…

"Beautiful," Jake uttered the words, causing Esmé to turn quickly, embarrassment at being caught sending heat through her cheeks. Her fiancé cleared his throat and leaned against the doorjamb. "Why do you have those clothes on?"

She glanced at the box, which had Jake's gaze wandering over to it. "It was a gift from someone who…died recently."

"The old man?"

Her temper prickled at the causal way he'd mentioned Luke. "His death meant something to me. I'd appreciate you showing some respect," she snapped.

He nodded at her temper, but didn't appear bothered by her outburst as he lifted the box and tossed it from the bed. A heavy clunk sound was made against the hardwood flooring just before the box landed.

She frowned and went looking, finding a small, silver hair comb. A poppy detailed the silver before the teeth of the comb.

"You are being ridiculous," Jake snapped.

"You just told me I was beautiful." She raised a brow.

Jake blushed. "You are."

She sighed, moving over to the mirror. "I can't marry you, Jake," she blurted it out. Removing her engagement ring, she watched his reaction through the mirror. He seemed resigned, as though he'd expected it.

Placing the ring on the chest of drawers, she slowly turned back to the mirror and took hold of her long hair. She twisted it up onto the top of her head and slowly inserted the fancy comb, admiring herself.

She still wondered about the locket Luke had placed in her hand during their first meeting—and the meaning behind the gift, as she placed the chain around her neck. Holding the locket in her hand, she went to open it.

It flipped open the moment she touched the aged clasp. Esmé gasped in delight, her shock apparent as she stared at herself and Luke Carlisle. Seconds later, her head started spinning…buzzing in her ears...her balance was off...she was falling...

Jake questioned, "Esmé?" His voice sounded like he was in a tunnel so far away.

"Esmé?" Jake yelled.

She tried to focus on him, but the room wouldn't stop spinning, and spinning, and spinning...

Jake stared at the spot where Esmé had been standing mere seconds before, and...and, she was gone. Vanished. He fell to his knees on the floor. Where had she gone? One minute she'd been looking at the locket, opened in her hands, and the next...*gone.*

He blinked a few times, wondering how many drinks he'd had before coming home to tell Esmé he wanted to separate. She'd beaten him to it. At the reminder a laugh burst from his lips because—for once—they'd been on the same page.

But what he'd just witnessed was beyond his comprehension. Had that been her way of getting back at him for the lousy mood he'd been in for months? Some trick she'd discovered in a magazine or something. It had to be. Hadn't it?

Except what he'd seen with his own eyes was his ex-fiancé vanishing. She'd literally gone poof. Like a puff of smoke!

Jake shook his head as he clambered from the floor and stumbled into the living room. He poured himself three fingers of good old Irish whiskey, and dropped into his favorite armchair while he thought about what to do. He really didn't want to think about what had happened in the other room. However, he couldn't stop. He'd seen her vanish with his own eyes. If he told anyone, they'd think he'd gone crazy. He'd have to agree with them.

How was he going to explain where she'd gone? They'd lock him away and throw away the key if he told them the truth. And they might do the same if he didn't.

CHAPTER 9
APRIL, 10TH 1912

Noon

The moment her head stopped spinning, Esmé still kept her eyes tightly closed. She listened to the sounds around her; birds squawking, running feet, string instruments off in the distance. People shouted farewells, and cheers of happiness continued to cause her head to throb. Esmé was terrified to open her eyes because everything felt different. Her senses were on high alert so she concentrated on breathing through her fear, which was when the smell of briny seawater hit her nostrils.

Her heart fluttered and she felt a faint thread of hysteria trying to push through. She quickly shut it all out before it could take over...she ran Luke's words over and over in her mind, "I love you. Come back to me," and she discovered that it helped to focus her thoughts on him and the desperation she'd felt behind his words.

Minutes must have gone by, but she didn't really care because something told her she was no longer in New York. She was certain the world she'd known in 1987 had just disappeared, and she was no longer a part of that. She just knew it to be true... and, as the horn of a very large ship blew, shivers raced down her spine in excitement.

In that moment, she forgot all about being afraid, as she slowly peeled her eyelids open. She'd known she was half lying down on something, and now she realized it was a wooden deck chair with a rough brown blanket thrown over her legs.

Her body trembled as she swung her feet over to the side and slowly stood. With the need to peer over the side of the ship, she moved closer to the open deck. Esmé's heart pounded as she gripped the ledge in front of her and peered over the side. Her eyes trailed way down to the dock below and in astonishment, Esmé realized that she was somehow on board the Titanic as it pulled out of Southampton in *1912*.

The dock was littered with people from all social classes who had come together to watch the huge ocean liner sail from England on its maiden voyage. She spotted men with notepads in their hands, scribbling words or drawing pictures that would become part of history.

It suddenly hit Esmé that she was witnessing an historical event—an event that would become more historical in five days time, when the RMS Titanic split in two and ended up at the bottom of the ocean.

Her hand reached up and her fingers ran over the locket. Buzzing started in her ears, like a swarm of bees. She quickly dropped her hand to her side. The locket must be the trigger, but how was that possible?

As people jolted her to look over the side of the ship as she left the docks, Esmé mind was in turmoil. Until she'd woken up on board, she'd never thought anything like this was possible. Luke had known, which meant the small bits of information she'd learned about him—and herself—had to be true. Had they really met and fallen in love on board this ocean liner before disaster struck? If so, how did she end up back in 1987 while Luke spent years waiting for her in order to send her back to him?

Backing away from the side, Esmé glanced around, wondering what she was going to do next. She couldn't stand around in an evening dress; other passengers were already looking at her oddly. Others wore day clothes while she stuck out like a sore thumb in the pink gown. It also gave no protection from the elements as she shivered when a particularly strong gust of wind whipped through her clothing.

Her eyes followed the length of the promenade deck, observing men and women as they walked along, some with children trailing behind them, some with nursemaids. When they passed by Esmé, more odd looks were thrown her way, even though they were still polite and tipped their heads in greeting.

Esmé closed her eyes as she pressed a hand to her stomach, trying to move away from the unease wrapping itself around her. With a deep breath, she opened her emerald green eyes and began walking.

She didn't know where she was going, or where anything was located on the ship, but she knew she had to find Luke, and maybe locate her cabin. That thought stopped her in her tracks. Fifteen minutes ago, she'd been in her apartment in New York back in 1987, now she was on board the Titanic in 1912. How would she even have a cabin?

"I should have really done more research," she muttered to herself, and then laughed. She hadn't exactly expected to land in 1912 when she'd placed the locket around her neck. Her departure had been swift and sudden from the...*future*.

"Pardon me, Miss, are you all right?"

Esmé blinked a few times at the crewman who had stopped in front of her. He was of medium-height, and his smile was wide, the teeth strikingly white in his tanned face.

"I...I think I'm a bit turnaround. I can't quite remember where my cabin is."

He tipped his head to the side, deep in thought. "Then tell me what number your cabin is, and I'll direct you back."

She bit her lip and felt sick inside, as she admitted, "I'm afraid I can't remember. Perhaps if I gave you my name you'd be able to find out for me." She hesitated. "I'm so sorry about this. I'm not usually so forgetful, but all this is very overwhelming." She waved her arms around, giving the young man a pleading look.

"You stay right here, and I'll go and quickly find out. What is your name?"

"Esmé Rogers." The young man nodded kindly and hovered. He quickly pulled one of the rough brown blankets from a deck chair and wrapped it around her shoulders. He spun on his heel and took off running in a light jog.

She was bewildered by his abrupt action, but smiled nevertheless. He'd looked more boy than man, maybe seventeen—he was kind.

The blanket was rough, but it kept the chill off, which she appreciated as her cold shivers slowly ebbed.

She walked back and forth and smiled when he came running back. "I've found your stateroom." He grinned. "You are really close so let me take you back there." He indicated with his body language that she should follow him.

"Thank you." Esmé glanced around but didn't really have time to take anything in with the boy moving so quickly. He probably wanted shut of her, even though he seemed to have an air of enthusiasm about him. "I really appreciate this," Esmé said kindly.

"It's no trouble, Miss." He stopped and unlocked the cabin door. "This is yours. It's on the Promenade Deck, Miss."

"I'll remember now. I'm so sorry to have troubled you."

"Do you have a key Miss?" He smiled, gently.

"No, I don't...I'm sorry, I seem to have misplaced it." Esmé fretted.

"It's no worry Miss, take this one." With a smile, he handed over the key he held in his open palm.

Did she tip him?

What with?

"Oh!" she gasped when the door opened fully and the grandeur of the room became apparent. Mahogany paneling covered the lower part of the walls, with thick wallpaper on the top half. A large bed was to one side of the room and looked so comfortable she yearned to just lie down on top of it. A lovely sofa in red and gold was up against the opposite wall with an armchair close by. A side table sat beside the chair, and in the center of the room there was a table for two.

"It's a beautiful stateroom, Miss. The finest in the world," the boy informed her, reminding her that he stood there.

She blinked and stared at the boy, wanting to be alone, but she couldn't let him go without a tip.

Glancing around the room, she spotted

what looked like a purse, so she quickly dashed over and sighed in relief when she found some money. She had no clue what any of it was worth in the time period she was in, so she took out one large silver coin, fifty cent, and passed it to the boy.

His eyes lit up as he backed out of the room. "Thank you, Miss. If you need anything else, please ask for John."

She hid her amusement at his delight over the money. She had obviously given him more than the standard tip. "I will. Thank you again."

He looked ready to say more before he quickly disappeared, the door closing behind him. She sagged into the plush sofa, although it wasn't quite as comfortable as she'd expected.

12:30PM

Her eyes slowly trailed around the room while she tried to explain why her name was on a stateroom, and why there were *things* in the room? Esmé had done the impossible, traveled through time. Although she knew there would never be an explanation as to the how or why, she hoped there would be one for her current surroundings.

Whoever Esmé Rogers was in 1912, she obviously had money. The stateroom must have cost a small fortune. Nothing had been spared in the elegance of the room, and apart from the gentle rolling of the liner, the silence was welcoming.

Slowly moving forward, Esmé let the blanket drop from her shoulders to the sofa. A door to the left of the room held her attention, but as she put her hand on the cold, smooth, steel handle, it wouldn't move. Locked.

A connecting room—maybe?

The other door in the room held a dressing area that overflowed with clothing, shoes and accessories. Amongst the items she spotted some more corsets, which she wouldn't even contemplate wearing. The dresses were in abundance, separated into day and evening, much to her relief. The shoes seemed to be laid out in rows, starting with the palest pink, and then gradually deepening in color. She was obviously a neat freak.

The small door to the side led to a bathroom, the vanity littered with items. Curious as to what women used in this era, Esmé moved over and picked up a small pot of what she presumed to be moisturizer. There were a couple of small pots, both in gold. One held bright red powder, and another, a pale pink color. A small pot of poudre de riz sat in a small green container. She smiled, delighted with her find, and especially as it was the very one she used herself back in 1987 to set her make-up. The packaging was different. Opening the last pot, she discovered something black, which she took for mascara. "I've no idea how to apply you," she muttered to the pot, fastening the lid.

Her gaze lifted to the regal mirror; for the first time since she'd opened her eyes on board the ship, she felt as though she could breathe. Her stomach was still in knots but, the fact that she looked the same, just slightly bewildered, helped to calm her nerves.

What would be her next move? Would Luke know her, or would they be meeting for the first time? What would she say to him? Should she try and warn the Captain of what would happen? He'd probably think she was crazy. Who wouldn't?

She wandered back into the main room pondering where to start. Perhaps by changing into a day dress? Turning slightly, the door to her room started to open, and with her heart in her throat, she stayed frozen as a teenage girl appeared in the doorway. She wore the uniform of a maid.

"Oh!" the girl gasped, her hand going to her chest. "I've been looking all over for you."

"You have?" Esmé replied, startled. "Um, I forgot where the stateroom was."

The girl closed the door behind her, and moved closer. "I take it you really like that dress if you're wearing it now?"

"Um," she glanced down before meeting the girl's gaze, "I love this dress, but I think I should change."

"That would be a good idea." The young girl giggled.

Esmé stared in surprise. She let the young girl fuss around her and watched while she took a cream day dress out from amongst the selection in the closet. Tiny peach flowers covered the skirt part of the dress, and the top was plain cream with fine lace. It was lovely, but she had no idea who this girl was, and didn't know how to ask when they obviously new each other.

"You'll look so pretty in this," the girl sighed.

"It really is a lovely dress, um, um..." Esmé waved her arm around.

"Violet. I'm eighteen, Miss," the girl volunteered, a frown on her young face.

Esmé tapped her forehead. "I'm sorry. I must have gotten colder than I thought outside, and your name escaped me."

Violet laughed. "Oh, not to worry, Miss. After all, we only met before you boarded the ship, so just over an hour ago. Your parent's solicitor employed me. God rest their soles."

"That's right," Esmé mumbled to herself, swallowing hard.

Behind her, Violet started undoing the

dress she wore, and when Esmé stepped out of it, the girl gasped. "Your corset has disappeared."

Esmé couldn't help herself and giggled at the pure astonishment because there wasn't a corset beneath her dress. She chuckled. "It's, um…" her eyes trailed to the closet and the other torturous corsets.

"Miss, you have to wear one. What will people think?"

Another giggle popped out of her mouth. "Unless I get undressed in front of them, I don't see how they'll know I'm not wearing one."

"But…but, everyone wears one. You have to as well." Violet dashed over to the closet and tugged one free.

Esmé shook her head when the young girl faced her with the torturous contraption in her hands. "I'm sorry Violet, but I'm not wearing that or any other corset. I wish to be able to breathe, and I won't be able to in that thing."

Amused at the shock on Violet's face, Esmé turned and twirled in her undergarments. "Let's get me into the dress so we can go and explore."

"You," Violet hesitated, "you want me to explore the ship with you?"

"Of course I do!" Esmé frowned. "You're the only friend I have on this ship." The minute she uttered those words, she wondered whether or not they were true.

"Well, maybe I could hold your jacket or something. We could watch what is going on in the water. The Titanic pulled the New York toward us, and we narrowly missed colliding," Violet informed her. She wouldn't meet Esmé's gaze while she slipped into the beautiful day dress.

Esmé had forgotten the story she'd read about the Titanic and the New York. If she remembered correctly, there was also another ship too that was nearly pulled toward the Titanic...*Oceanic*!

With her thoughts elsewhere, Esmé only just caught sight of Violet as her hand reached for her neck. She quickly ducked out of the way and cleared her throat. "This necklace never comes off. Ever." She smoothed her fingers over the delicate jewelry. "I can't explain, but never remove it." She smiled to take the bite out of her words.

Having a maid felt odd to Esmé. All her adult life, she'd had to do everything herself. With that in mind, she turned to the young Violet. "I have an idea." Clapping her hands together, Esmé took the girl by the arm and dragged her into the closet.

"Let me see. We're about the same build, although you're a little bit shorter than I." Esmé sorted through the clothes and came up with a peach day dress. It was plain in color but had embroidered flowers on the skirt and sleeves. "This is very you."

She smiled and turned to face the pale Violet. "I don't understand, Miss."

Esmé shook her head and shoved the dress into Violet's arms. "I'll wait in the bedroom while you get this on."

"What? Miss, no! I can't wear your clothes. They'd put me off the ship."

"Nonsense! You're employed by my parent's solicitors, right?"

Violet nodded.

"So how can they put you off the ship when they employed you for me? I don't have a problem with you. I may if you don't put that dress on and accompany me to lunch, followed by a walk in the fresh air on the promenade?"

Esmé didn't wait for Violet to decide, she just shut the door with the girl on the other side.

She couldn't remember the last time she'd been so excited.

2:40pm

The promenade deck was freezing in the brisk weather, even with her thicker day dress on. Esmé was glad Violet had reminded her of that. Her smile was firmly in place and she couldn't help the amusement she felt when she glanced at Violet who looked bewildered and doe-eyed, but still very pretty. Wisps of dark brown hair framed her young face.

She had a feeling that Violet would have been more comfortable in third class, but that wasn't going to happen. The girl had the small room close to Esmé's stateroom. At least Esmé would know where to find her.

She was positive that Violet was going to be a good friend. If only she could get her to act like she belonged.

Heaven knew, Esmé wasn't the best person to give etiquette lessons to someone, but they could have fun trying.

"Violet, you need to walk beside me with your head held high." Esmé took her own advice. Glancing out of the corner of her eye at the girl, Violet looked ready to bolt back to the safety of her room. "Look confident, even when you feel sick with nerves and fright. Don't let anyone see how you're really feeling."

Violet slowly lifted her head and Esmé smiled. "Don't look at your feet again." Esmé winked. Turning forward, she missed a step when she noticed the man walking toward her in a light-hearted conversation with another man, who had a beautiful woman on his arm.

The man with the couple was tall, dark, and handsome, looking at him made her heart pitter patter in her chest. His broad shoulders filled his jacket and even as she felt a tug on her sleeve, she couldn't look away.

Luke.

"Miss," Violet hissed. "Miss." She tugged on Esmé's sleeve again and tried to get her moving.

"I can't move," she whispered.

Just as the three newcomers were about to pass, the man, whom Esmé couldn't take her eyes from, turned his head, his eyes met hers.

His flow of speech suddenly went silent and he stilled, even as the man and woman continued walking.

Olive and Matthew?

"Luke, do you know this lady?" the man asked, nudging Luke.

Esmé snapped out of the trance she'd been in and found Luke doing the same. He cleared his throat and offered his hand, "Luke Carlisle," while holding her gaze.

"Esmé Rogers," she breathed, her heart taking flight toward him. As soon as her trembling fingers touched the warmth of

Luke's outreached hand, she felt as though she was where she was supposed to be. Her palm slid softly along Luke's and when he enclosed his fingers around her hand possessively, she hoped he would never let her go.

The other man cleared his throat. "Luke, where are your manners?" He frowned, his gaze jumped between Esmé and Luke.

Blinking a few times, Luke slowly released her hand. He placed a protective hand on the small of her back and kept her close to his side.

The man and woman continued giving them strange glances while Violet stayed off to one side. Luke changed his hold, and reached for her elbow. His fingers stroked the tender underside of her arm sensuously.

"Esmé,"—hearing her name on his lips was as though she'd just taken a bite of the finest chocolate—"let me introduce you to my brother, Matthew, and his wife, Olive."

She'd been right. Her heart sank—she knew that they wouldn't be alive in five days. The urge to warn them to leave the ship in France, for all of them to leave in

France, was on the tip of her tongue. But after a moment's pause, she said, "It's nice to meet you both." Esmé moved closer to Luke, or did he move closer to her? She couldn't decide. "Let me introduce you to my close friend, Violet..." her voice trailed off as she once again met Luke's gaze.

"Violet Gibson." Esmé let out a relieved laugh when Violet spoke up.

"I'm sorry, my mind has momentarily deserted me," Esmé apologized, feeling a blush working its way onto her face.

Matthew laughed. "You're not the only who is having trouble remembering their manners today." He pointedly looked at his brother, who blushed. "Perhaps, you both would like to join us at our table tonight for dinner?" Matthew invited, gentle lines of laughter bracketed his mouth and creased the sides of his dark eyes. He was a dark figure, big and powerful, and almost as tall as Luke.

Esmé turned her face up to Luke, who appeared to be holding his breath for an answer.

"We'd loved to. Thank you for the invitation," Esmé replied.

"Luke, we have business to finish discussing," Matthew urged.

"It's been a pleasure to meet you both," Olive offered. "I look forward to not being the only woman at the table this evening." She smiled brightly, her bluish-green eyes full of excitement. She looked more delicate and ethereal than anyone Esmé had ever met before and there was a gentleness about her. Her lovely caramel brown curls were windblown as they all stood and chatted.

Luke moved his arm up to her shoulder in a possessive gesture before he reluctantly let go. "This evening," he said. "I'm not going to be able to concentrate on business now that I've met you," he whispered for Esmé's ears only.

Her fingers fluttered to her neck where her pulse throbbed. "I look forward to seeing you again."

Matthew cleared his throat, except this time he grabbed hold of Luke's elbow and tugged him along with them.

Luke's eyes stayed on Esmé until they

disappeared inside. Violet moved to stand in front of her, a brow raised. "What was that you just said before about letting people see how you're really feeling? Or did I misunderstand that lesson?" she teased.

Esmé opened her mouth to reply before she snapped it closed. She held back the laughter bubbling inside as she realized the amusement in the whole situation. "I take that back, but only if you meet the handsomest man."

"He is handsome, and he certainly found you pleasant." Violet grinned, but then she frowned. "I don't think I've ever seen two people meet quite like that before. Are you sure you've never met him before?"

"We haven't." To all intents and purposes, they hadn't met before because, when they had met in 1987, Luke had aged. "I think I need a nap."

"Me too. It's exhausting being your friend," Violet moaned and spoiled her complaint by giggling. "The truth is I am having more fun than I've ever had before."

"I'm glad." Esmé slid her arm through Violet's as they went inside.

Moments later, they heard footsteps thundering down the promenade, and, turning swiftly, they watched as Luke came dashing through the door looking a bit disheveled.

He took two, strong strides toward Esmé while she felt Violet slipping away behind her. He pushed stray tendrils of hair away from her cheek, and Esmé leaned into him lightly as he tilted her chin up.

His large hands cupped her face tenderly. "I've never, in my life, been so forward with a woman but there is something about you. I need to touch you to make sure you're real. I don't understand what is happening to me." He laughed. "I'm not making sense, but, just this once, for a moment in time, I need to do this in order to take my next breath." His lips brushed lightly against hers as he spoke, before he claimed her mouth in a surprisingly gentle kiss.

Esmé couldn't think of anything but the feel of Luke as he caressed her soft lips with his own. Her hands trembled as they reached up, sliding around to the nape of his neck.

Unsteady, Luke raised his mouth from hers and gazed into her eyes, letting her see everything she'd made him feel.

"We were meant to be together," Esmé whispered.

Luke swallowed and stepped back, his breathing harsh. "This evening," he uttered the words like they were a declaration.

"Yes."

He left as suddenly as he'd appeared.

"You could at least play hard to get," Violet murmured, a smile on her lips.

Esmé covered her mouth with trembling fingers, as a soft smile slid across her lips. Turning to her friend, she couldn't hide her joy. "He's my soul mate, Violet."

6:30pm

Esmé stood on deck beside Violet, the young girl bubbling with excitement at seeing Cherbourg, France. All Esmé could see was the way Luke had held her gaze just before he'd kissed her. The taste of him still lingered headily on her lips. In remembrance, Esmé lifted her hand to her lips, smiling softly.

"Are you going to play hard to get tonight, Miss?" Violet asked, her eyes alight with amusement.

Esmé laughed. "I have no intention of playing hard to get. The man has me, which I think he knows."

Violet sighed, loudly. "They do say this is the ship of dreams, so I guess dreams do come true."

Esmé turned and faced the young girl at the wishful note in her voice. "Dreams are sometimes all people have. Don't ever give up on them Violet."

"None of my dreams have ever come true."

"Tell me what you would wish for *if* you believed in dreams?" Esmé asked, moving closer.

Violet's eyes glazed over for minutes, until she turned her whole body toward Esmé. Her eyes glowed with excitement. "My wish would be to stay in New York and make something of myself." She became animated with her hands as she talked. "I'd love to make ladies' dresses, but not just make them. Design them."

"Then dream, Violet."

Her face fell. "I won't be allowed to stay in New York."

Esmé frowned, and tilted Violet's face up to her so she could watch her closely. "What do you mean? I thought you worked for me?"

"I do, Miss. But I've been engaged by a family who are sailing on the Titanic from New York."

"Hmm," Esmé muttered and smiled. "We'll see." The minute the words left her mouth, she felt the color draining from her face. Did Violet survive the sinking?

"Miss, you've gone white."

She struggled for breath. "From this point forward, please call me Esmé. We're friends now, after all." Esmé stood and smoothed her hands slowly along her pink dress and over her hips. "I'm fine," she reassured Violet, who didn't look all too convinced.

Forcing a smile, Esmé said, "I just know

something." She fidgeted with the bracelet around her wrist. "I don't know how to tell anyone what I know or even if I should tell someone."

What would happen if she told the Captain and he actually listened to her without thinking she was crazy? Would it change history? Would that mean she stayed in 1912 with Luke, or would she still end up back in 1987?

Her head hurt from it all. As far as she was aware no one had ever been able to time travel regardless of the movies she'd seen about it. But she was here. She was in 1912 so it was possible. The science of it, she would leave to someone else.

The bugler, playing 'The Roast Beef of Old England' broke into her thoughts. He was letting the passengers know dinner was about to be served.

Her belly fluttered with nerves. "It's time."

Esmé smiled. Violet looked so pretty in the evening gown she'd been reluctant to wear.

They walked nervously through the ship toward the dining saloon.

Esmé caught her breath when she found herself at the top of the grand staircase. She'd only ever seen black and white photographs of the masterpiece during a documentary. The shipwreck had only been discovered in 1985, and reports said the staircase hadn't survived the sinking.

To be standing here, looking down, gave her a funny feeling, one that made her head spin. She was grateful to have Violet with her, because, once again, the girl helped to pull her back to the present and settle her.

Reaching out, Esmé placed her hand on the banister and slowly started to descend with Violet beside her. Violet looked so excited, it was as though she would burst with it. Esmé knew that feeling, which intensified tenfold when she turned to head into the saloon, and found Luke standing off to one side.

Her breath caught in the back of her throat as everyone else disappeared into the background. All she could see was Luke as he moved toward her in his dinner suit...his eyes not once leaving hers.

"Esmé," he breathed the words. "I've been waiting for you. You look beautiful." His fingers slid sensuously over the skin of her arm where her long, white gloves finished while his eyes dropped to her red lips.

At that moment, she blurted the truth, "I'm afraid."

Luke frowned and touched her trembling lips with a finger. "You don't need to be afraid of me. I would never hurt you."

"No, I'm afraid that I'm going to hurt you," she admitted, tears hovering on her lashes. "I don't want to hurt you."

He held her steady gaze. "Let me worry about myself." He smiled and offered her his arm. "I'd like to accompany, Violet, and yourself into dinner."

Moments passed, and then butterflies took flight in her stomach as she slipped her hand through his arm and took hold of his forearm, his muscles tensed under her gentle touch.

He cleared his throat and gave an encouraging smile to Violet. She smiled and gingerly placed her arm through his other.

"I'm a lucky man tonight, having two beautiful ladies to escort me into dinner." He smiled at Violet who beamed up at him, and then he turned his attention to Esmé.

When he looked at her, she felt as though she'd known him all her life, and his gaze seemed to sink into her. Regardless of them only just meeting, she knew she would do everything she could to stay in 1912 and spend the rest of her life with Luke Carlisle.

She offered him a loving smile and watched as his eyes danced with delight before they were interrupted.

"Can I take your photograph?" a small man enquired, looking to weigh significantly less than the heavy equipment he had over his shoulder. "It won't take but a minute."

Violet quickly backed away while Luke positioned them just so. It took a few moments for the photograph to be taken. When Luke started to lead her away, she glanced over her shoulder and saw *RMS Ti-*

tanic printed on the glass of the door they'd been stood beside of.

The plated photograph.

Her eyes showed sadness while her stomach fluttered with unease.

"Is everything all right?" Luke asked, concerned.

She turned to Luke and smiled. "I think it is." And with Luke looking at her, she truly believed it was.

He gave her arm a gentle squeeze and then held his other out for Violet who'd suddenly reappeared.

As they moved through the elegant dining saloon, she felt her equilibrium settle in her beautiful surroundings. The blue of the floor featured a red and gold pattern, and the walls were painted in white with Jacobite wooden paneling. Leaded-glass windows having been lit from behind to conceal the portholes.

When they reached their table, Matthew stood in greeting while Luke made sure Violet sat next to a young man, who he'd introduced as James Calder. James was a tall, handsome man with touches of humor around the mouth and near his eyes. He wore his black hair short, but it appeared as though it would be unruly unless tamed. His gunmetal gray eyes didn't move from Violet, who had a rosy blush to her cheeks.

Esmé returned Olive's knowing smile as Luke seated her beside him. He moved closer and stretched his arm across the back of her seat.

Esmé enjoyed the heat from his body and, daringly, she moved slightly so that her thigh pressed against his. His large limb trembled before she glanced across the table when his brother cleared his throat. "I trust you rested well this afternoon?"

"We did, thank you. I hope we get to explore more of the ship tomorrow. Maybe see the coast of Ireland as we dock at Queenstown in the morning."

"We've never been to Ireland," Olive offered with a smile. "Matthew had business in London, so we left our young child back in New York. It was a lot easier than bringing him with a nanny. He's safer too."

Matthew laughed. "I keep telling Olive that we're on an unsinkable ship." He patted her hand in affection. "We'll be home with our boy soon. We've missed him very much."

"I've missed having him to spoil," Luke commented, his smile wide.

"How old is he?" Esmé asked.

"William is a cheeky two year old," Olive offered. "Do you have family in America, Esmé?"

Luke played with a tendril of hair at the nape of her neck and his touch sent goose bumps down her spine, which made breathing difficult.

She glanced at him and found herself unable to look away from his mesmerizing stare as he offered her a lazy smile.

"Um," she stuttered turning back to the other occupants of the table as they gazed expectantly toward her, "family...um. I don't have family in New York, but I do have distant family in Boston." Or did she? "My parents died so I'm traveling to New York." She smiled and glanced at Violet who was blushing at the attention from James. "My good friend Violet is accompanying me. We're going to have new adventures."

COME BACK TO ME

"Hopefully not alone," Luke added quietly.

Esmé turned her gaze to him. "If that is an invitation for you to show us around, then I gladly accept."

He grinned. "It most certainly was an invitation."

"Perhaps, I could invite myself along," James commented, his gaze still on Violet, who appeared smitten.

Violet stayed silent, so Esmé replied for her, "We'd love for you to join us, Mr. Calder. Wouldn't we, Violet?" She reached out over Luke's leg with her foot and gently kicked the other woman to get her attention.

Luke burst out laughing. "I think she's in agreement," he commented with a chuckle.

Dinner started being served and Esmé was too distracted with the closeness of Luke to even pay attention to what she ate. Every glance, every slight touch, filled her heart with excitement.

Once the meal was cleared away, the orchestra started playing and, when Luke pushed away from the table, he held his hand out to her. "Please dance with me, Esmé."

"Where?" she whispered.

"There's a small, open space." He smiled.

She reached out, lacing her fingers with his and let him lead her to the dance floor. His arm slipped around her waist and he squeezed her affectionately while he held their joined hands close to his chest. "I've wanted you in my arms since we met. I can't believe it was only a few hours ago. It feels so much longer."

"I agree." Suddenly overwhelmed with emotion, Esmé dropped her forehead to his chest, and felt him place a soft kiss on the top of her head.

"Look at me, Esmé," he asked. "Please, I want to see your beautiful face. I want to see the way you look at me because no one has ever looked at me that way before. As though I'm all they see, or want, or need."

"You are all I see," she tipped her face up to his and their lips ended up a breath apart, "and, I want you. I need you. I want so much with you, and…and, it's scary considering we've only just met."

"It is scary, but now I've found you, I'm not prepared to let you go."

"You might not like me when we get to know each other."

Luke pressed her completely against his taut body. "That will never happen," he said forcibly. "Never, Esmé."

His eyes burned as they focused on her lips before he lifted his gaze to hers. "You believe me?"

"Yes." Esmé smiled and moved slightly away from his body. The heat seeped through her, and Luke needed to calm down.

"I need some fresh air." He stopped dancing. "Walk with me?"

Esmé nodded, enjoying the feel of his hand on the small of her back as he escorted her from the dining saloon and up to the promenade.

"I can breathe again." Luke commented and laughed. "I always feel as though everyone is watching me." He mock shuddered. "I'm so glad that I have met you. You made it bearable."

"You being with me makes everything

that's happened to get here, bearable." Esmé touched his cheeks, the skin cold beneath her fingertips. "I'm so afraid that we'll have everything, and then it will all be taken away from us."

Luke frowned, caressing her face with his eyes. "Why do I get the feeling you know something?"

"These sudden and intense feelings I have for you, frighten me," she tried to explain, without telling him the truth just yet. There would be another time for the truth, and hopefully he wouldn't think she was crazy.

She reached out, and pressed a hand lightly to his chest, sighing when he pressed his palm to her hip. His free hand moved recklessly to her neck, holding her softly as his thumb caressed over her pulse. "You're unique, Esmé Rogers," he whispered against her lips.

Just as they leaned closer, chatter from behind Luke pulled them slightly apart. Luke coughed and as he watched Esmé shiver in the cold night, he took his dinner jacket off and wrapped it around her shoulders, keeping his arm around her.

Esmé settled against him with her face pressed against his chest. "Tell me about Luke Carlisle, and why he was on business in London?"

He chuckled softly. "Our father started an engineering company sixteen years ago. Matthew and I, run the six factories. One of them is in England. Just outside of London. It turned out that one of the parts our father started out manufacturing is needed inside the engine of an automobile. It can't run without it."

"That's absolutely amazing," Esmé tilted her face up to Luke's, wondering why she hadn't known that before.

"It can be a nuisance and messy." He smiled. "But it's a very lucrative business so I have no complaints." His tone softened. "If I hadn't been on business then I never would have met you."

Leaning down, he slowly curled his fingers into the back of her hair.

Esmé felt her knees weaken as his mouth slowly descended. "I'm going to kiss you now." His last words were smothered with her lips, and they were both shocked by her eager response to the touch of his lips.

She thrust her fingers through his thick, black hair as he roused her passion while his own grip grew stronger.

Shivers of delight followed each touch as his kiss became urgent and exploratory, before he left a trail of fire along her jaw, grazing her earlobe with his warm mouth.

"I need to take you to your cabin," he whispered, "and leave you safely behind the door until I collect you for breakfast."

"Mmm, I like the breakfast idea," she mumbled, while she had a burning desire, an aching need, for another kiss from his swollen lips.

Luke groaned and slowly put her away from him, his hands going to her shoulders. Her hands caressed down his chest and, at his swift inhale; she quickly snatched them back, wrapping them around her stomach.

"Where is your cabin?" he whispered, breathing harshly.

"Close. This floor."

He groaned. "So is mine," he admitted chuckling. "You've been sent to torture me."

She led the way inside while Luke kept his arm around her shoulders. As they approached her cabin, Luke volunteered, "This one is mine, just so you know where to find me if you need anything."

Her surprised laugh startled him, so she explained, "I think we have adjoining rooms."

"What?" His eyes widened before he closed them, deeply inhaling. "Please keep your side locked. I seriously don't trust myself to be alone in a private room with you." He gulped and saw Esmé to her door. "I'll knock at eight for breakfast."

After a kiss to her cheek, he quickly moved away. Minutes later, she heard his door open and close.

The huge grin on her face stayed as she quickly let herself into her cabin, where she ran and dived onto the bed, rolling to her back.

"I love you, Luke Carlisle," she whispered, her hand covering her mouth to hold in the giggle of excitement.

It didn't bother her one bit that she was acting like a teenage girl with her first crush. She felt giddy, and she couldn't wait to see him in the morning. Her eyes moved to the locked door separating their staterooms. She'd never been more tempted to unlock a door before.

She wouldn't.

Her eyes started to drift closed when she started to wonder what Jake and Sienna, back in 1987, thought of her disappearing.

CHAPTER 10

1987

Sienna nearly jumped out of her skin when the doorbell chimed. It was loud and unexpected. From her position at the dining room table, she couldn't make out who it was, so placing her pen down beside her notebook, she moved closer.

"Who is it?" she shouted through the door.

"Um, Jake Preston. I'm looking for a Sienna Taylor. She was a friend of my fiancée, Esmé Rogers."

Her heart raced because she'd wondered what had happened to her new friend. She hadn't been able to get in touch with Esmé since she'd left with the box of clothing.

"Is everything all right with her?"

"No," he moaned. "She's disappeared and I wondered if you knew where she was. I mean," he laughed, "one minute she was in front of me and the next she wasn't. I know I sound crazy, but I need to talk."

The minute she heard about Esmé, she panicked and quickly unfastened the locks. When she heaved the heavy door open, she was startled to find Jake Preston looking less than immaculate. When she'd seen him in the restaurant the night she'd first met Esmé, he'd been neat as a pin, now he wore scruffy jeans, a sweater with a hole in the sleeve and a head of disheveled hair. The thought that she preferred him this way popped into her head, which she shook away. No way would she think of her friend's fiancé in that way.

"I'm Sienna." She stepped away from the door. "I think you better come in."

"Thank you." He sighed in relief and hovered while she closed the front door.

"I have a pot of coffee in the dining room if you'd like a cup?" Sienna offered,

COME BACK TO ME

leading him through to where she'd been sitting, pondering.

"I wouldn't say no." Jake smiled, taking the offered seat.

Sienna joined him after she'd topped her own cup up with the steaming liquid. They sat together in silence for a long time, until Jake started talking.

"We'd been arguing, and she'd just put an end to our engagement." He sighed. "I'd actually been out drinking, trying to work up the courage to do the same. I think Esmé thought I was having an affair." He laughed. "I'm not a man who would ever be unfaithful to anyone, no matter how unhappy I was. I just figured it was easier letting her think that. Maybe she'd end our engagement quicker. She never did because I don't think she cared enough about me to be bothered." He shrugged.

Sienna kept quiet. She'd gotten the same impression from Esmé, so he was on the right track, but he didn't need her confirming it.

"That night, I came home, and she had on an old dress. I flung the box it had obviously come in to the floor and out flew a hair comb thing." He swallowed and held her gaze. "She put the comb in her hair, and then fastened the necklace around her neck. The one with the locket that wouldn't open."

Leaning forward in his chair, and in a controlled voice, he continued, "She vanished. She had no trouble opening the locket. She gasped when she took a closer look, and then that part of the bedroom, where she stood, went hazy. When it cleared, she was...gone." Jake threw his hands in the air.

"Where did she go?" Sienna asked, more to herself than Jake.

"I don't know, which is why I'm here. The doorman gave me your message to her, a couple of days ago. So here I am."

"I don't know what to think." Sienna felt all the blood rushing around in her head because, surely, Esmé hadn't discovered a way to go back to Luke?

"You know something. I can see it on your face." Jake watched her carefully.

"What I know will sound as crazy as you do about her just disappearing."

"After what I saw, I'll believe anything. Trust me on that." Jake's eyes begged.

Sienna nodded, and admitted, "Luke was a survivor of the Titanic. He never spoke about it to me or anyone as far as his son, William, knows. Luke, apparently, became a recluse not long after he arrived back in New York on board the Carpathia. William said there was speculation that he'd met a woman on board and fell in love with her. The conclusion was that she'd drowned, but, more recently…"

"Sienna, do you have my reading glasses?" William interrupted as he walked into the room. He glanced up from the paper in his weathered hand. "Oh! I'm sorry. I didn't know you had a visitor. My apologies." He was a slim man with neatly trimmed snow-white hair.

"It's okay, William. Come and meet Esmé's…"

"Friend," Jake finished.

"Esmé?" William asked, confused.

"She held your father's hand when he

died. You met her afterward and at the funeral," Sienna reminded. "You'd been out at the club when she was here asking about a photograph your father gave her."

"Ah!" He tapped his forehead and stared at Jake. "This isn't as good as it once was." He shook his head, a frown darkening his features. "Esmé," he mumbled to himself. "I know that name." He joined them at the table.

Sienna passed him his glasses, which he ignored, lost in thought. She turned back to Jake, and whispered, "I'm sorry. He forgets things."

Jake smiled. "It's okay...Do you mind continuing?"

"I can do that." She glanced at William and back to Jake. "Before Luke died, he told Esmé he loved her. He told her to... 'find me in the past'. He left clues and things for her, and we were even starting to believe it was possible..."

"Esmé!" William burst out, smacking his palm on the table, grinning. "I thought my memory was failing me again."

"I don't understand." Sienna watched

him.

"Esmé was the name of the woman my father was in love with."

Unable to form any words, Sienna stared at him.

He continued, "Both of you come with me."

If it hadn't been for Jake, she'd have stayed in the dining room, but he pulled her out of the chair and kept his hand on her arm as they followed the old man through the house and into an office.

"He told me about Esmé when I found a small box buried in one of his drawers. It contained a locket. He was so angry I'd stumbled upon it. But then he told me he'd fallen madly in love with Esmé, a woman he'd met onboard the titanic. When he talked about her, it was the first time I'd ever seen my father cry. It broke my heart to see how distressed he was over her loss. I'd actually forgotten, until last week." He laughed. "I can't remember what I did yesterday, but I remembered that from when I must have been around five-years-old." He shook his head sadly.

Jake pulled Sienna down to the sofa with him, just as her legs were about to give way. They both watched as William flicked through a large box of papers.

"What are you looking for?" Jake asked.

The older man froze. "This." He pulled out a large, square photograph. "I found this last week, which jogged my memory."

He held it out and Jake took it. Sienna was too shaky to even think straight let alone hold something so delicate.

Jake turned it so they both could look at it, and sucked in a harsh breath when he saw his ex fiancée staring back at him.

"The inscription on the back says Luke Carlisle and Esmé Rogers. It's also dated."

Jake flipped the photograph.

April 13th, 1912.

"It was taken on the outside deck of the Titanic." Sienna frowned. "How did it survive?"

Jake flipped it back over. "It's been folded at one time. See?" Jake trailed his finger along what looked to be crease marks. "I think he may have had this restored. I don't understand how this is even possible. That's Esmé." Jake laughed. "Although, I never thought it was possible for someone to just vanish either."

"But this is proof she made it back to him, Jake."

"Why would she go back to him if she knows she'll die a few days later? That doesn't make sense."

"Now I'm confused so I'll leave you both to get on with it." William disappeared, closing the door on his way out.

"Maybe," Sienna answered Jake, "she thought she could change history." She shrugged.

"Or maybe she thought it was the easiest way to leave me," Jake offered.

Sienna, blinked. "Don't think that way." She placed a hand on his arm. "Esmé has been obsessed with Luke and finding answers from the moment she met him. She said he was familiar to her, but yet she had no memory of why."

He sighed heavily. "So, what do we do now?"

"I honestly don't know."

CHAPTER 11
APRIL 11TH, 1912

11:20am

Luke gazed at Esmé across the card table while she tried her best to concentrate on the game of bridge. The only game she could remember how to play, that Violet, Luke, and James, also knew how to play. She wasn't doing very well since she was too distracted by the handsome man who wouldn't stop looking at her. He had her all upside down and swimming in an assortment of nerves.

"I think we should take a stroll along the promenade very soon so that you can see

Ireland as we arrive in Queenstown, which I believe you said you wanted to see," Luke reminded her.

"I'd love that." Esmé turned to Violet and raised a brow. The girl blushed. "I'm sure James wouldn't mind escorting you."

James laughed. "I'd love to." He pushed away from the table. "I think we should forget about cards as I don't think anyone is really interested. Let's take the stroll now." He held his arm out to Violet, who looked just as excited.

"Alone at last," Luke commented, shuffling his chair closer. "I've been waiting for this moment since you walked out of your room this morning." His fingers brushed her cheek as he leaned in, giving her a soft kiss against the lips. "So precious."

She slipped a hand to her stomach, holding on tightly so she didn't reach out to him. By the look in his gaze, he knew exactly what she wanted to do. "Are you planning on behaving today?" he whispered.

"In public, I will," she teased.

Luke paused for a moment before he threw his head back and laughed. A few heads turned in their direction, but she paid them no heed.

"I think you are going to be trouble in more ways than one," he admitted, getting to his feet. "Shall we."

She took his offered arm and allowed him to lead her to the promenade. "I hope Olive is feeling better. I missed her at breakfast."

With mirth in his gaze, he leaned close. "Between you and me, I think she's pregnant." he grinned. "I love babies! What about you?"

"I haven't thought about children, but I think I'd like some."

"Hmm," Luke laughed. "How many is some?"

Esmé smirked, and watched him from the corner of her eyes. "I was thinking ten had a nice appeal."

He coughed, and spluttered. "*Ten?*"

Laughing, Esmé, agreed, "One or two would be just fine." She patted his arm. "I take it you're planning on being the father?" Her lips twitched as she met his serious gaze. The smile slowly fled from her face.

"Yes." Luke's one word made her head spin as he urged her to keep walking. "And don't think I haven't noticed that you always change the conversation to me when I ask you something personal."

She knew he would notice something so obvious, she just didn't know what to say. So she gave him something, "I'm originally from Boston. My father was a banker before he was killed in an accident with my mother." All of that was true. "I will tell you everything soon, even though I'm afraid you'll think I'm crazy when I do."

His hand cupped her jaw and tilted her face up to his. He gazed into her eyes and then brushed a soft kiss across her lips. "I promise not to think you're crazy." He quickly kissed her again before moving her over to the side of the ship. "Ireland."

She gasped, a smile edging her lips. "I've always wanted to visit Ireland, so to actually see it fills me with excitement."

"I'll bring you back here one day," Luke whispered into her ear, his arm keeping her anchored to his side.

Her happiness faded at the thought of

one day. Would she still be with Luke, or would she somehow end up back in her time?

"Have I scared you?" Luke asked, picking up on her distress.

Reaching for his hand on her waist, Esmé intertwined her fingers with his, and then she reassured him, "Talking about having a future with a man I've only just met should terrify me, but I find it doesn't. It makes me impatient," she turned her face up to his, "to have that future."

Luke groaned and snapped his eyes closed while he caught his breath. "Please watch Ireland," he groaned, opening his eyes. "If you continue to look at me that way, I'm going to embarrass us both."

Esmé stepped between him and the side of the ship. She looked out as they anchored approximately two miles outside of Queenstown, known in 1987 as Cobh.

Feeling unsteady, Esmé took his hands into hers and placed them around her midriff, their fingers holding the connection between them.

They stood for a long time, watching the

small boats and ferries sailing toward the ship. Neither said anything, and neither wanted to break the silence of the loving and caring embrace they shared.

It wasn't until the passengers actually started coming aboard from the tender ferries that Luke moved her away from the side of the ship. "I could hold you in my arms all day, but, perhaps, you'd like a cup of tea to warm you up?"

"That would be lovely." Esmé felt bereft when Luke dropped his hands from around her waist. She smiled widely when he cupped her elbow to lead her away from the promenade.

As soon as they stepped inside the lounge, Olive and Matthew waved them over. "Please join us," Olive invited, sitting on one of the sofas in the spacious area. It reminded Esmé of a hotel lobby, except it was more extravagant and had been decorated lavishly like the palace of Versailles.

Luke waited until she'd sat beside Olive before he sat in an armchair next to his brother—the two immediately engaged in conversation.

Olive smiled. "I'm sorry we missed eating breakfast with you. Matthew went and brought some food back to the room and ate with me." She smiled softly at her husband. "He worries about me."

"He loves you," Esmé added, with a smile of her own.

"I have a feeling we're going to be seeing a lot more of you when we're back in New York. I'm excited for that, and for you to meet William. Let me show you a picture of him." She searched her large purse and pulled a small photograph out of a chubby two-year-old.

Olive sighed. "I can't wait to be home."

Sipping her tea, she remembered meeting William back in 1987. He'd been in his seventies, was in good health, apart from his loss of memory. She'd only really spoken to him at Luke's funeral.

Tears came swift and sudden and she couldn't blink them away.

The startled look on Olive's face let her know she couldn't hide her distress from Luke, who quickly snapped his head in her direction.

"Esmé?" Luke wrapped an arm around her shoulders while Olive passed her a white handkerchief.

"I'm sorry," she sniffed, trying to pull herself together. "Seeing the picture reminded me of my friend's little boy. He died just before I sailed." She hoped they would leave it at that because she couldn't tell them the truth about their fate. Dabbing at her eyes, she patted Luke's cheek. "I'm fine. I really am." She smiled to reassure him. "And Olive, you have a lovely son. I'm sorry I broke down like that on you."

"Oh, nonsense." She patted Esmé's knee. "These things happen."

Luke still watched her closely, but said nothing more before he became engrossed in the conversation with this brother again.

"Your friend, Violet, seems to be having fun with Mr. Calder," Olive mentioned. "We saw them playing croquet not too long ago."

Esmé chuckled. "Violet is an amazing young woman—full of dreams. I really hope they come true for her one day."

"I have a feeling that Mr. Calder is going to be whisking her away with him once we get to New York." Olive fanned herself. "I'll sure have stories to tell Matthew's mother. First you, turning Luke's head, and then young Violet with Mr. Calder. You'll love Luke and Matthew's mother. At first impression, she appears strict, but she isn't."

Excitement grew in Esmé as she listened to Olive talk about New York. Of course, she knew her way around *her* New York, but not the one of 1912. She turned her head to face Luke in profile, and her heart leaped with joy at his closeness. She'd do anything to spend the rest of her life with him. She never wanted to leave his side. She wanted seventy-five years with Luke, not four and half days.

7:00pm

"What were you thinking earlier?" Luke asked.

Esmé frowned wondering what he was referring to.

He saw her confusion, and offered,

"With Olive over tea? You were talking and then you turned and stared at me." He smiled. "I love you looking at me, it was such a soft look, and I wondered what you were thinking right then."

Olive had noted the way she'd looked at Luke, and had offered a raised brow once Esmé had started up the conversation again. They'd both ignored it, but she'd known Luke wouldn't.

She moved closer, and felt his response in the way his chest rumbled in pleasure. With a teasing smiling on her lips, she admitted, "I was admitting to myself that I wanted to spend the next seventy-five years with you."

He stumbled briefly, and cleared his throat. "Is that right?"

"Hmm." She smiled at the couple walking upstairs, as Luke led her toward the dining saloon. "I hope you don't mind."

"No," he squeaked, clearing his throat again. "I don't mind." His face gradually split into a delighted grin. "I don't mind at all."

The dining saloon seemed to be where everyone met to eat and gossip. So many rumors had been spread since she'd been on board the ship. A lot of which, she found out from Violet, who somehow managed to know everything.

"You seem cheerful tonight," Matthew commented to his brother.

"I have a beautiful woman on my arm, why wouldn't I be cheerful?" Luke winked at Esmé. "Besides, you look just as cheerful." He grinned. "Anything to tell me, brother?"

Matthew blushed bright red while his wife and Esmé chuckled behind their hands.

"What's so amusing?" Violet asked, joining them on James Calder's arm.

"I think my brother has an announcement to make." Luke grinned, putting Matthew on the spot.

Esmé tugged on Luke's hand as he finally took his seat beside her. "Leave him alone." She shook her head, amused.

Matthew sat and took his wife's hand. "Olive and I are going to be proud parents again."

"I knew it!" Luke slapped his thigh before he leaned forward and kissed Olive on her cheek, offering congratulations to his brother. "It's good to always be right."

"Don't let him fool you, Esmé," Matthew teased. "He's not always right, I am."

"Oh, stop," Olive begged, laughing. "When they both get started, it can take a while for them to calm down.

"Hmm, I've seen them a time or two," James added before he turned his attention to Violet.

Luke whispered into her ear, "I'm glad you're here with me, Esmé."

"Me too." She smiled, her hand slipping to his thigh for mere seconds before she moved it back to her own.

"After dinner, we'll watch the stars," he suggested.

"I'd like that."

"So, Esmé," Matthew interrupted, "whereabouts are you heading once we reach New York?"

Nerves fluttered in her belly at the question because she had no idea where her final destination was supposed to be. She certainly knew where she wanted it to be. "Well, I think my final destination has changed since I boarded the ship," she admitted, her eyes finding and holding Luke's.

He gave her a dark look before a grin split his face. "If I have my way, Matthew, you'll be seeing a lot more of Esmé."

A robust laugh burst from between Matthew's lips. "I knew that, of course, I just wanted to hear it confirmed. I think Olive would like to have a friend."

Frowning, Esmé turned to the other woman and searched her face. Questions teased at her mind, but she would wait for now to ask them. She didn't want to embarrass Olive in front of the others.

"I'm hoping that Olive will show Violet and I the best places to shop."

"I'd be delighted to. We'll take afternoon tea at The St. Regis," Olive said, leaning over Luke, she then whispered, "It's owned by John Jacob Astor. He's a passenger onboard this ship with his young wife, Madeleine. She's pregnant and the gossip is running rampant."

"Olive," Matthew warned.

Olive winked and sat straight in her chair. "Sorry Luke," she grinned, "Didn't mean to lean over your food." Turning to her husband, she said, "Esmé might not have known."

"Everyone knows." Matthew exchanged a look with his wife while Esmé leaned against Luke's side.

He leaned closer and was taken by surprise when Esmé placed her lips gently against his cheek, and whispered in his ear, "Can we really be together in New York?"

"Yes," he replied without any hesitation.

"Then that's what we'll do." After one more peck to his cheek, Esmé finally noticed how quiet Violet had become.

James ate his meal but kept glancing at Violet, and that's when it hit Esmé what was wrong. The poor girl thought she *had* to sail back to England.

Reaching out, Esmé placed her hand over Violet's to get her attention and, when she had it, she told Violet, "You are in charge of your own destiny, Violet. Plans that you had when boarding this ship can be changed." Esmé glanced at Luke with a soft smile on her face, and admitted, "Mine have."

She felt the warmth of Luke's hand on her thigh, squeezing it gently at her words. She held Violet's gaze while the young girl pulled herself together.

Esmé turned to James and saw in his gaze just how much he liked Violet.

"I think both of your destinies changed when you came aboard this ship," Olive observed.

"Very astute, dear." Matthew waved down a waiter for his wine to be topped up. "My brother's, certainly, has." He grinned. "I wish they'd hurry up with the rest of the food so we can celebrate our good news with the finest cigar."

Beside her, Luke groaned. "I hate those smelly things."

"You always have, but you can have a glass of whiskey instead, although I plan on having both."

"Don't you dare get all smelly and drunk, or you'll be sleeping on a deck chair out on the promenade," Olive told her husband.

"Now dear, you know those old wooden things play heck with my back."

Luke laughed. "Then you know what to do to prevent that, brother."

A yellow dessert was placed in front of Esmé. It reminded her a bit like the bread and butter pudding her grandmother used to make with the raisins she could see around the surface.

Curious, she leaned into Luke. "What is this called?"

"Waldorf pudding. Try some, it's really very good." He offered her a small amount on his spoon.

A small blush worked its way up her neck and to her face, but she accepted the offered sweet, savoring the delicious flavor as it slipped down her throat. "I haven't had it before. It's lovely."

Luke cleared his throat and turned back to his dessert while Esmé quietly ate hers.

It wasn't long before Matthew insisted both Luke and James join him for a drink.

Luke brushed a kiss against her ear, and whispered, "I'll come and find you later."

Her smile lit her whole face while Luke's eyes glittered with longing.

"He's so besotted with you," Olive commented. "James with you as well, Violet." She clapped her hands together. "You have both met two amazing men. Of course, I'm not impartial because Luke is my brother-in-law, and James is a family friend. It's just that neither of them have ever shown a great deal of interest in any of the women my mother-in-law has tried to shove at them." Her smile slipped and she grew solemn. "Please don't hurt them."

"Why would we hurt them?" Violet asked.

"What she means is when we get to New York, not to disappear without a trace when I think both Luke and James want to keep us with them." Esmé stared at Luke's back. As if he knew her eyes were on him, he turned his dark head, curiosity in his gaze. "Luke wants me with him, and that's where I intend to be. I'd be willing to fight my destiny for a chance to spend my life with him."

"Oh." Olive sighed. "I'm so glad you feel that way about him. He feels that way too, he can't keep his eyes off of you, or his hands for that matter."

"I'd have said his lips," Violet mumbled under her breath.

Esmé met Violet's gaze and laughed. "I would have to agree with you both. I feel as though I've known him for years." She became serious. "Not just a day. He's inside of my heart." She pressed the palm of her hand against her chest, as tears hovered on her lashes. "And I know he will be until the day I die."

"You've made me cry." Olive dabbed at her eyes with a soft handkerchief, while Violet looked to be in a daze.

"I think you've just described the way I feel about James." Violet shook her head and sat back in the chair. "I'm in love with James."

A gasp from behind them made their heads turn to find James in shock with a wide, silly grin on his face. Not one word was spoken as he helped Violet from her seat.

Esmé watched the two lovers disappear.

"Bless my heart." Olive pressed the handkerchief against her chest. "How old is she?"

"Eighteen."

"Esmé, please walk with me." Luke appeared, as did Matthew to attend to his wife.

"I'll see you both tomorrow." Esmé wrapped her arm into Luke's.

"You will, and thank you for this evening Esmé. My mind is totally at rest." She glanced at Luke before her smile landed on Esmé. "Good evening."

As soon as they headed away from the dinning saloon, Luke asked, "What was that all about with Olive?"

Esmé gave him a cheeky laugh. "Wouldn't you like to know?" she teased. "It was women's talk."

"Is that so?" His lips twitched. "What if I told you I can read lips, and I really hope I read yours correctly?"

Shocked, Esmé narrowed her eyes at Luke. "You are teasing me?"

He laughed. "Let's just say I think it would be wise if I drop you off at your stateroom and say goodnight."

"Hmm, I don't think I'm ready to say goodnight just yet." Esmé squeezed, Luke's arm. "Will you take me to see the stars?"

Luke placed his arm around her shoulders as soon as they found themselves on deck, then he wrapped his dinner jacket around her. "You'll freeze otherwise," he commented, keeping her close as they walked to the side.

"I'm glad it's a clear sky tonight," Esmé said, delighted. "I think we both should choose a star and wish upon it."

"Pick one." Luke settled behind her with his arm around her midriff as they gazed out across the moonlit night to the quiet whoosh of the ship moving through the water.

She wished for a lifetime with Luke.

"I've picked one and made my wish," Esmé turned and gazed up at Luke. "Your turn."

After a long glance at Esmé, Luke stared out to sea and closed his eyes. Moments later, they opened and focused on Esmé.

"I hope our wishes come true," he whispered.

"Me too." Esmé buried her face against his throat, breathing a kiss there, which caused her body to tingle from the contact.

Luke mumbled against the top of her head, "I really need to see you to your stateroom." He kissed her ear, cupping her face in his large hands. "You're under my skin, Esmé Rogers."

CHAPTER 12
APRIL 12TH, 1912

3:00pm

"Miss?" Violet muttered. "Esmé."

"That's better." Esmé twirled in the pale pink dress she wore; thanking God she'd managed to avoid the dreaded corset again. "What can I help you with?"

"Do you think I'm spending too much time with James? I should be working for you."

Esmé shook her head. "I'm really happy for you Violet. I want you to be happy and if that means spending all of your time with James, then I'm all right with that." She took

Violet's hands into hers. "I don't need help to dress, bathe, or tidy my room." Esmé laughed. "I've been doing all that on my own for years."

"It just doesn't feel right." She clarified, "Me leaving you alone."

"Violet," Esmé said exasperated. "All my time is spent with Luke, which is the way it should be." She smiled at the thought of him as warmth filled her body. I want to talk to him and get to know him better, and I wouldn't be able to do that if you were with us." She stood. "You must find it easier being with James without me around, right?"

"I guess."

Esmé rolled her eyes. "Violet, enjoy yourself with James. I hope that, one day, we're both lucky enough to be married and best friends in New York." She grinned and twirled around the room. "I love this dress."

"It really is very pretty." Violet looked down to her own dress with a secretive smile. "This is James's favorite color."

Esmé gently cupped the young girl's face. "You are so pretty Violet, and please, I beg you, from this point forward, forget about everything before walking on board this ship. You are Violet Gibson, and what's mine is yours." Almost giddy, Esmé added, "I'm so excited for the future, Violet," before her smile slipped.

Violet tipped her head and frowned. "If you're excited, then why do you look so sad?"

Sighing, Esmé sat in the armchair and rubbed at her cold arms, suddenly chilled. "Nothing is simple for me. I can't really explain it and, if I could, I'm not sure if anyone would believe me."

"Then talk to Luke. He'll help you." Violet smiled. "He loves you."

"As James does you." She returned Violet's smile, and jumped up with a sudden thought. "I know what I'll do." Esmé quickly kissed Violet on each cheek, grabbed her jacket and left the stateroom.

In a rush, she quickly dashed toward the Purser's office, only to be pulled up short. "John!" Her hand clutched her chest in surprise. "You startled me."

"I need to talk to you, Miss." He glanced around, his words urgent.

"Can we talk later?" Esmé questioned. "I need to talk to the Purser."

John shook his head. "I need to talk to you before you talk to anyone."

She tilted her head to the side and frowned, staring at the boy; she wondered why he was so adamant. "I don't understand."

"I know." He sighed. "But, if you don't talk to me first, you will regret not listening."

She opened and closed her mouth. "Um, all right."

He nodded, relieved. "Let's move out of the way. We can't be overheard."

More curious than ever, Esmé hoped Luke wouldn't catch them talking and get the wrong idea.

Once they were alone, John turned to her. "You can't tell anyone what you know?"

"About what?"

He tugged at his hair. "If you tell anyone about the impending disaster, you will vanish back to where you came from. Everyone here will have no recollection of you, but as punishment for trying to interfere with the future, you'd remember, and the disaster you tried to stop, will still happen."

"Oh!" She sat down heavily on the bench behind her legs.

She stared at him, her mind spinning. "I was born in 1734," he answered her unasked question. "I seem to be permanently stuck at seventeen. I only know the future of the Titanic because I've been here before, which makes no sense, but it's the truth. The second time I was onboard, I tried to warn the Captain, just like you are trying to do. That's how I know what will happen to you if you tell anyone."

"This is all too much to take in."

"Yes, it is. I can't explain and I don't even know what I've done to go through time, but it keeps happening to me. I'm stuck. I don't want that to happen to you."

"So I can't tell the Captain?"

He shook his head.

"Or Luke." She covered her mouth with a small hand to keep the cry at the back of her throat inside.

"No one." He shook his head again. "This

happens no matter what you do or say. The only difference is that, if you stay quiet, and providing you and Luke get back to New York, you can have a life with him. You would have nothing if you try and tell someone what you know."

She sat in stunned silence, and then asked, "What about afterwards? If I admit to Luke I knew about it and where I'm from, once the Titanic has sunk, will I stay or be sent back?"

"As long as you don't interfere with history then you'll be okay. You just can't tell anyone what you know about the future before it happens." He sighed. "No one can interfere with history." He hesitated as though he wanted to say more. Then he added, "But the course hasn't been firmly set for anyone." He smiled, wryly. "You set your own future, Esmé, that hasn't been set in stone, yet."

Her heart beat franticly while she tried to understand what was being said, but all she felt was confusion. "Are we the only people?"

John stared at her for a moment. "No, I

don't think we are. You're just the only one I've met."

"How did you know?"

"I only suspected at first, but I've watched you. Sometimes you appear lost, out of your element. I was going to knock on your stateroom just now and I overheard you talking to Violet about not knowing how to explain something. I took a chance."

"And you were correct."

"I'm glad I was," John said. He tipped his cap and quickly disappeared.

"I am too," she whispered.

Esmé sat for a long time while her heart cracked wide open. It turned out she had no control over what was going to happen in only a few short days. All these people would lose their lives in two days, and she couldn't do a single thing about it. It made her angry that she couldn't change anything.

"I've looked all over for you," Violet said, placing a coat around her cold shoulders. "We've all been worried, but a crewmember told me where to find you. It was strange but, never mind, I have you now."

"Luke?" Esmé whispered, letting Violet lead her back to her stateroom.

"He's worried. He's on the deck below looking for you. Let's get you warmed up, and then I'll try to find him."

Esmé nodded—slowly starting to thaw from the shock of her discovery. "I'll be all right, Violet." She turned and pleaded with the other woman. "Please, don't fuss. I really am okay." She smiled in reassurance. "Go and spend time with James."

Violet slowly nodded. "If you say so."

"I do, and I really will be all right getting to the stateroom." She leaned forward and kissed Violet on the cheek. "Thank you for looking out for me."

Violet smiled and ran off back to James.

Esmé clutched at her stomach and sagged behind the door once she reached the safety of her stateroom.

After her talk with John, she felt on edge and didn't know what to do about it. She couldn't talk to Luke either, which she'd hoped to do. She hated not being honest about where she came from or what she knew.

. . .

7:45pm

"You gave us quite a scare this afternoon," Matthew commented. "Thought you'd fallen overboard."

"Thanks for the reminder," Luke mumbled, in a surly mood.

Esmé glanced at him but he avoided her gaze. There had been too much commotion once word had gotten out that she was back in her stateroom. Once everyone had disappeared, she'd knocked on the connecting door, but, if Luke had been in there, he'd ignored her.

At the table, she could feel the anger coming from him. Finally having enough, she stood, surprising everyone including Luke. When his gaze finally lifted to hers, she asked, "Please walk with me. I have something to say."

Without a word to the others, Luke took her arm and led her out onto the promenade.

"I'm sorry, Esmé. You had me worried. More than worried if I'm truthful. Yet, you gave no real explanation. I thought your feelings were growing for me, like mine were for you."

Esmé swallowed hard. "My feelings for you are profound Luke. It's not that I don't want to tell you because I do. Desperately. I just can't. But, I promise you, when we are in New York, I will explain everything to you. Everything Luke. I just can't tell you until then, and I'll explain why then as well."

She grabbed the front of his dinner jacket tightly. "I need you to trust me until then."

He watched her carefully; the slight smile on his lips told her that he was going to trust her. "You promise to tell me everything?"

"Once we reach New York, I will tell you everything. I'll answer any questions you have. I will still sound crazy and have no real way of proving anything to you, but I will tell you every single thing I know."

"Then, as curious as I am, I will trust you

to talk to me once we reach New York." He leaned forward and kissed her forehead.

He offered his arm and led her further down the promenade. "Are you hungry?"

"Not really. I was too worried about you not talking to me to have an appetite."

"I was too concerned for you, to have one." He chuckled. "We make a right pair, huh?"

"I love us together." She snuggled her face into his arm as they strolled along the deck, when Esmé asked, "Would you like to come back to my stateroom for a nightcap?"

Luke pulled her over to the side and forced her gaze up to his. "Are you sure us being alone together is wise?" He quickly pressed a finger to her lips as she opened her mouth to speak. "I know what I want and that is you in my life for the rest of my days. However, I don't want there to be any gossip about you because of me."

Wrapping her fingers around Luke's wrist, Esmé tugged his hand away but kept it in hers. "I want the same as you do, but I want to be able to relax with you without others watching. I just want to have you all to myself for a little while."

He pressed his forehead to hers. "Then we'll open the adjoining doors so no one is aware. I need to protect you."

"And you," she added.

"I'm not bothered about my reputation, only yours."

"Hmm," she sighed, moving closer.

"Let's head there now." Luke cleared his throat and took Esmé's hand, placing it on his arm. "We're being watched," he muttered.

Within minutes, Esmé was inside her stateroom. She took a deep breath in an effort to calm her nerves, then she turned the key into the connecting door to let Luke in. She knew people would deem it wrong, but never had anything felt more right. Her heart danced with excitement. When she opened the door, and saw the heart-wrenching tenderness of his gaze, a tingling in the pit of her stomach took flight with butterflies.

"To receive such a look of loving tenderness from you fills me with joy." Luke offered a wry smile. "I'm glad that we're alone to receive it." Taking her hand into his, he pulled her into his stateroom. "I have whiskey if you'd like some."

"No, I'm fine." She laughed. "Although I am nervous, so maybe it will put me at ease."

"Oh, Esmé. I promise you have nothing to fear from me." He poured them both a finger of the fine Irish liquid, and indicated with a nod of his head for her to join him at the small table.

"I'm not afraid of you per se, I'm afraid of what you make me feel, and because of that, I'm afraid of what I may do." Esmé looked away before Luke took her chin gently into his hands and turned her back to face him.

"That took a lot of courage to say out loud."

She acknowledged his words.

"So let me tell you I feel the same way about you. We only met two days ago and I do believe there is something else at work." He laughed. "I've never been so compelled to be with a woman before—never Esmé.

But with you, it's like I'm afraid to take my eyes off you. I have this desperation to bind you to me so you'll always be with me. It's almost as though I'm afraid you're going to disappear. The truth is I've fallen in love with you."

"You have?" she gasped. "I love you too." Without another care or thought, Esmé launched herself out of her chair and into Luke's lap and waiting arms.

She'd dreamed of being crushed by his embrace, and now here she was. It made her heart jolt and her pulse pound. The longer he held her against him, the more she ached for the fulfillment of his lovemaking.

She felt the movement of his heavy breathing against her and then heard his whispered words, "Marry me, Esmé." His breath was warm and moist against her face, and her heart raced when their passion filled gazes met and held. "You're mine, and I want you to be my wife, the mother of my children, and my partner throughout our life. Please tell me *now* if you don't want that." He stood, pulling her with him, his hands locked against her spine.

Everything she had started to wish for back in 1987 was coming true. Although it terrified her, she was going to believe the words she'd spoken to Violet, about being in charge of their own destiny.

One large hand moved up to gently cup her cheek, worry etched on his handsome face. She offered him a loving smile. "I love you, Luke Carlisle, and I want to be all those things to you; your wife, the mother of your children, and your partner throughout life. I love you." Standing on her tiptoes, she touched her lips tenderly to his.

Luke's kiss was slow and thoughtful, until their tongues touched, then he took over the kiss, his mouth covering hers hungrily. Suddenly, she was lifted into the cradle of his arms. His kiss sent the pit of her stomach into a wild swirl of desire and the taut body against hers trembled as their passion grew.

Just as suddenly, his mouth pulled away. Panting harshly, he placed Esmé back onto her feet before he took a step away from her, turning his back. She could see the harshness of each breath he took, which seemed to be a struggle. It was tough for her, too. She couldn't catch a breath from the desire coursing through her blood.

The need to touch him, soothe him, became overwhelming so she moved up behind him, her arms locked around his waist. She rested her face against his back and sighed. "I love everything about you. And I love how you make me feel," she admitted, exhaling a long sigh of contentment.

Luke squeezed her hands still hovering on his stomach before he slowly moved them away and turned to face her. He captured them back up with his larger ones and admitted, "My passion for you knows no bounds, but I won't lay with you until we're married." He kissed her knuckles. "The Captain can marry us."

An amused smile on her face, she teased, "So quickly?"

Luke smiled. "We love each other, and when we disembark from this ship, I want you on my arm as my wife." He smirked.

"You are a romantic man, Luke Carlisle. You fill my heart with so much love, so please arrange our wedding for as soon as you can."

He kissed the tip of her nose. "I will talk to the Purser first thing in the morning and see if he can arrange it with the Captain."

Esmé tugged him along with her to sit on the side of his bed. The occasional jolt from his thigh brushing her hip, made her skin tingle. She dropped her forehead to his chest with a sigh of pleasure. "I've never had anyone really love me before." She tilted her face so she could hold his gaze. "I feel so much love when you look at me, touch me. I never want that to fade."

"I promise you it will never fade," he exclaimed with intense pleasure, softly kissing her waiting lips.

A powerful feeling of relief washed over her as she admitted, "I can't wait to become Esmé Carlisle." With a quick kiss, she jumped to her feet. "I want everything with you Luke. I don't just want to be a stay-at-home wife. I want to be with you in every sense of the word."

"That's what I want, Esmé." Luke followed her to her feet, removing his jacket.

He placed it on the back of a chair and fiddled with his bowtie before he finally had it opened and off. He tugged at the collar of his soft pleated dress shirt, and opened a couple of studs. "I finally feel as though I'm not choking. I hate these stiff collars."

Esmé's eyes went to the skin he'd revealed between the open collar and her body ached to touch him there.

He groaned. "I hate to end this evening, but if you stay much longer, I won't be responsible for my actions." Even as he spoke, his eyes raked boldly over her before he snapped his eyes closed.

She took pity on him. "I'll go. I hope you'll accompany me to breakfast?"

"Always, my love." He reached out and lightly stroked along her cheek before he pulled his hand away. "Always," he mumbled.

Before she threw herself into his arms again, Esmé quickly went through their connecting doors, locking hers behind her. The temptation was there to leave it unlocked, but she couldn't do that to him.

CHAPTER 13
APRIL 13TH, 1912

7:45am

Esmé stepped out of her stateroom and quickly looked around when someone hissed further down the hallway. She turned and found John motioning for her to join him.

Checking to make sure Violet wasn't approaching, she quickly made her way toward him, out of sight of other passengers.

"I wanted to make sure you were okay," he whispered, looking odd.

"I'm fine, but you're not. What's wrong?" Esmé frowned, watching him closely.

John sighed and paced in front of her before he stopped. "I shouldn't be telling you this, but," he paused, "there's a fire."

Her eyes opened wide in shock. "Where?"

"It's in the second and third sections, where they keep the coal. The men are talking about it been raging for three weeks. They finally have a handle on it today and feel confident it's going to be out soon."

"We shouldn't have sailed," Esmé muttered.

"No, we shouldn't have. Everyone involved has been sworn to secrecy. I only found out because I overheard the firemen talking."

"Has this happened when you've been here before?"

"This is the first time I've known anything about it, but I presume so." John looked sick. "The heat of the fire has weakened the hull, which I think is why the iceberg rips into it so easily. It may still have happened without the fire, but the hull is severely weakened now."

Esmé stared at the young man wondering if they could use it to their advantage and sabotage the ship. If they did something to make the ship stop or slow down, then surely they would miss the original timeline. History would be changed, and neither her, nor John, would have told anyone what they'd known.

"John," a sharp voice shouted. "You're with me."

The crewmember looked sharply at John before he gave her a cold glance.

"You better go," she whispered.

"I'll find you again," he said under his breath, running off.

She watched him join his crewmate. Grimacing when she noticed him being admonished for talking to her, a first class passenger.

8:15am

"Why are Luke and James so keen to talk

with the Purser this fine morning?"
Matthew asked, unable to hide the amusement in his gaze.

Olive took hold of his hand and
squeezed. "Now you behave yourself, and
stop embarrassing Esmé and Violet."

"I'll save it for Luke." He smirked.

Violet went a rosy shade of pink at being
teased, while Esmé tried not to give her excitement away.

The moment they'd arrived at breakfast,
both Luke and James had made their excuses before quickly disappearing. Esmé
couldn't wait for Luke to return with details
of their wedding. It was so fast, but she
knew her destiny lay with Luke. Right from
their first meeting in New York, she'd
known.

Olive cleared her throat, snapping Esmé
from her thoughts, as she changed the subject. "I'm so glad Luke suggested we eat in
here today."

They were in Café Parisien with its
French ivy-covered trellises that had an assortment of climbing plants, reminding

Esmé of the patio back home in Boston where she'd grown up.

A tiered buffet stand sat in the center of the room and contained an abundance of food. The china service sat on sideboards situated at each end of the room.

"It feels more relaxed in this room compared to the saloon." Olive gave a small smile in an effort to hide her grimace.

"Are you feeling well?" Esmé asked concerned for the other woman who looked white as chalk.

"A bit queasy, but nothing to worry about," she reassured, and took a bite from her small slice of buttered bread. "I just need something in my stomach, is all."

"The motion of the ship isn't helping. She'll be much better once we're on shore," Matthew added.

Esmé glanced at Violet from the corner of her eye, and saw her own excitement reflected back at her. Perhaps she could do with having a talk with Violet at some point during the day. Because one thing she did know about people in the early nineteen hundreds, they weren't as open as it had become in the eighties about intimate relationships.

Pulling her thoughts together, Esmé focused on her breakfast, a boiled egg and bread while she hid a yawn behind a hand. She'd had a terrible night's sleep after being with Luke and everything they'd talked about.

But her thoughts weren't just on what she felt for him, she couldn't stop thinking about what would be happening on the 14th. She was desperate to talk to Luke about what she knew, but she didn't want to risk her future with him. If John were to be believed—and there was no reason not to—then risking everything wouldn't change the outcome of the Titanic.

Esmé looked worriedly at Violet. Whereas her relationship with Luke had been written in the stars, she needed to make sure Violet was taken care of, and that James Calder was a good man.

She had so much on her mind that she hadn't noticed Luke approaching with a grin splitting his face. It matched the one she briefly caught on James's face.

Luke pulled out the chair beside her and, taking her hand, announced to the table at large. "The Captain will marry us tomorrow."

James announced. "And us."

"I just knew what was going on!" Olive grinned. "I just knew."

"Congratulations," Matthew shouted in his boisterous voice. "I think the men should sneak to the smoking room to celebrate after breakfast."

Luke chuckled. "You know I hate being in that room. I can't breathe."

"I promised Violet another game of croquet after breakfast, plus I also don't like that particular room."

"Boring," Matthew complained. "I'll think of something else." He wasn't to be outdone. "Eventually!"

Laughing, Luke said, "I'll leave it with you brother, but for now, I'm rather hungry."

He went to collect some breakfast while

Esmé finished hers, wondering if they would live to be married longer than a day.

"Violet, I think you, Olive, and I, should get together this afternoon to decide what we're going to wear for our weddings." Esmé squeezed Violet's hand. "I'm sure the men can find something to entertain themselves for a couple of hours."

"Oh, this will be fun!" Olive exclaimed. "I actually have just the dresses for the both of you." She grinned, more color in her face. "A friend of mine asked me if I could bring her back five different wedding dresses from London. They're originally from Paris. I'll tell her I misplaced two."

"A convenient friend," Matthew grumbled.

"Oh hush!" Olive blushed.

"No need. I will gladly reimburse you for Esmé's dress," Luke said between bites of breakfast, glancing at his sister-in-law.

"Of course, I will, too, for Violet's dress." James covered Violet's hand on the table. "I want to do this for my bride." He grinned. "You've agreed to marry me, so I need to thank you in some way."

"Oh! You don't need to thank me. I love you," Violet confessed, more confident than Esmé had ever heard her be.

"When I married Olive, I thanked her in another...*ouch!*" Matthew turned and glared at his wife while Olive ignored him, a blush coating her cheeks.

Esmé chuckled behind her handkerchief, and briefly met the amused gaze of Luke. She had to turn away before she lost it in a fit of giggles.

"Isn't it obvious, William was born nine months after our wedding?" Matthew added, pleased with himself at having had the last word.

Luke rolled his eyes. "I think I should commiserate with your wife for being married to you. Can't you keep anything to yourself?"

Olive groaned. "I think we need to change the subject." She smiled. "I also think that a few nights on the floor for my husband might keep his mouth closed." She turned to Matthew. "Wouldn't you say so, dear?" She patted his hand.

"I think the threat is enough," Matthew

grumbled. "I'd put my back out sleeping on the floor."

Luke threw his head back and laughed. "Showing your age, brother." He laughed.

"I'm only three years older than you." Matthew pointed his finger.

Luke chuckled and finished his breakfast in relative silence.

"If you'll excuse us," James stood, and helped Violet to her feet. "I'll return her after lunch so you ladies can have some fun without any interference from us men."

"I look forward to that," Esmé said, and quickly squeezed Violet's hand.

Violet beamed as she was led away. She looked absolutely besotted with James, which made Esmé's heart so much lighter. Knowing that the young girl, who she'd quickly taken a liking to, would be looked after, made it easier for her to concentrate on Luke. She was determined to have the life she craved with *her* man by her side.

She'd always thought there was something missing in her relationship with Jake, and now, after meeting Luke, she'd been right. With Jake, she'd never been totally relaxed. Always waiting for something to happen, never feeling at ease with him. From the moment she'd met Luke, even in New York, she'd recognized him. Since being on the ship, it was as though her whole being had recognized him as being hers.

CHAPTER 14

1987

"Do you think the time is passing at the same rate there?" Jake asked Sienna, but it was more of a spoken thought.

"If it passes at the same rate, then the Titanic has already sunk. It's been two weeks, Jake."

"We're assuming she appeared on the day the Titanic left Southampton. What if she went back before the Titanic sailed?" Jake watched Sienna and tried not to be distracted with how pretty she was.

He'd noticed Sienna that night in the restaurant, and had been horrid to Esmé, when it was himself he was angry at. He should not have had the thought about Sienna, or any woman, while with his fiancée.

Sienna blushed with Jake's gaze focused on her face. It was something she couldn't help, especially since she found him attractive. She dipped her gaze and cleared her throat. "We need to go back to the library and see if her name is on any of the lists for the ship." She sighed. "I should have done this before you came knocking at my door. I was just afraid, incase she was on the deceased one."

"It's hard to get my head around it. Obviously I want her to be alive, but if she is, does that mean she's going to stay there and spend seventy odd years with Luke. Does it mean our whole timeline thing is going to get screwed up? Or does she somehow come back with no memory, and that's why Luke waited all these years to tell her to go back to him?" Jake ran his hands through his hair. "I think I might be going crazy."

"Join the club," William said walking into the room.

"William!" Sienna jumped up, giving him a hug. "How was lunch with David?"

"Boring," he replied dryly. "He tells me the same thing every week." He dropped into an armchair. "I think he's the crazy one." He laughed. "So," he met Jake's gaze, "why are you going crazy?"

"Long story."

"Does it have something to do with that photograph I found the other day?"

"Very astute." Sienna moved to sit beside Jake. "Are you sure that's the only photograph you've seen with Esmé in?"

"I've been thinking about that." He tapped a finger to his lip. "I was two when I lost my parents, so I don't remember that time. But, I know that I've seen photographs taken around then. I'm just not sure where my father kept them. I've been looking." He threw his hands up and sighed. "I don't really know where else they could be...unless they're in the attic. Lots of dust up there."

"I'd forgotten about the attic." Sienna glanced at Jake. "Luke was constantly getting things moved up to the attic and I heard a lot of his personal belonging were put up there." Sienna swung her leg, her shoe dangling from her slim foot.

Jake forced his gaze away and concentrated on William, who gave him a knowing smirk before he cleared his throat. "I think you both should go up there and have a look around. I'm too old for those narrow stairs."

"I know where the door is, but I've never been in there before."

"A lot of history up those stairs."

Sienna glanced at Jake then back to William. "What is the earliest you remember?"

"I knew that was coming." He chuckled. "I have a vague recollection of being a child and playing with wooden blocks. Of my father, playing ball outside in the back." He tipped his head toward the back garden. "I do remember asking my grandmother why my father always looked sad. I used to think I'd done something wrong. Or that he was angry with me because he'd had to adopt me. She told me he wasn't angry with me, but I didn't believe her."

He shrugged, his gaze turned thoughtful. "What I told you before about finding a small box and my father explaining about the woman he loved, I felt sad for him, but I remember feeling relieved. I finally knew he wasn't angry with me, he was just sad." He frowned. "What does my father's Esmé have to do with the one I met at his funeral?"

"It's really complicated and you'll think we're both crazy if I tell you."

"Like I said before, I'm already crazy."

"William, if you can remember what you have, then you're not crazy."

William offered a wry smile. "Thank you for that."

"So," Sienna smiled, "I think I shall make you a cup of the lemon tea you favor, and then Jake and I will go up into the attic."

"You do that. Take some flashlights with you because I'm not sure the lighting still works."

"We will." Sienna stood, and tugged Jake with her. "Kitchen." She nodded with her head. "Tea coming up."

They dashed to the kitchen and Jake watched Sienna in silence while she made the tea. The scent of lemon reached his senses and made his nose twitch.

"What do you think we'll find up there?" he asked.

"Maybe more photographs of Esmé… some sort of proof she made it off the ship. I really don't know, but I'm impatient to get up there."

"I'm nervous. I want to believe she made it off the ship. But what if she didn't? Or what…" He dropped his face into his hands. "I don't know what, anymore. I just want to know how this all ends. It's constantly playing over in my head. I want to be able to move on," Jake made sure his gaze held Sienna's so she knew exactly what he meant before he continued, "and I need all this, to be over."

Sienna stopped what she was doing and moved to Jake. Wrapping her arms around his waist, her face tipped to his. "I understand what you're saying, Jake. I'm not going anywhere."

A cleared throat from the doorway broke them apart quickly and they turned to face William.

"I just remembered something," the older man said, thoughtfully.

"My father didn't have many friends, but there was one who visited every now and again when I was small. After her visit, he would be solemn for a few days before he'd snap out of it." He sat at the table in the kitchen with Sienna and Jake joining him.

"She was a bit younger than he was. When I was younger, she would visit with her husband. He died maybe twenty or so years ago. She still visited after he died but I never really got to know her well. She's in a residential home now. I think the lawyer called her when my father died." He tapped a finger to his lips. "Violet Calder!" He snapped his fingers. "My memory isn't as bad as I thought it was."

"You're full of surprises William." Sienna grabbed hold of his hand resting on the table. "Do you know how she knew Luke?"

"That I do remember. She boarded the Titanic in Southampton as a maid, and arrived in New York on the Carpathia with her husband James Calder, who was a family friend."

Jake stared at William, and asked, "Do you know how old she is?"

"Not really, but at best guess, I'd say she was in her nineties." He shrugged. "I can get you the address from the lawyer if you want to visit with her."

"That would be great William," Sienna mumbled, already forming questions in her mind, the attic forgotten.

CHAPTER 15
APRIL 13TH, 1912

2:30pm

"I trust croquet went well with, *James*?" Esmé drawled when Violet entered her stateroom, looking as though she was in a dream.

"Oh yes, Miss," Violet took a chair at the table, silly smile playing on her lips. "I'm glad you changed your mind about me being allowed to show what I'm feeling." She sighed.

Esmé laughed, amused. "I'm happy for you, Violet. Just please stop calling me Miss. It's Esmé."

Violet sat up straight, a sudden change in her demeanor, before she burst into tears. One minute she was happy, the next she looked like her heart was broken. "Violet?" Esmé asked, crouching at her feet. "What is it?"

"James doesn't know I'm your maid. I need to tell him before the wedding, so he can change his mind."

"Oh," Esmé smiled and encouraged, "I've seen the way he looks at you. He isn't going to change his mind when he knows the truth. Besides, the truth is you are my friend. You have never lied to him, so please remember that. I know you haven't told him how you came to be onboard this ship, but you also haven't lied either"

She nodded in agreement. "I've only told him the truth."

"Then, I don't think you have anything to worry about." Esmé patted her knee before she stood. "Olive will be here soon. Why don't you dry your face and stop thinking so hard."

Violet tilted her head. "Did you tell Luke what it was you had on your mind?"

That caught Esmé off guard and, with pain in her heart, she gently shook her head. "I don't know how to, but I have promised to tell Luke everything once we reach New York. There's a reason why I can't tell him beforehand, but he's told me he trusts me. Once we're on land and settled, I will tell him everything about me. No matter how big or small; I trust in our love that he will accept everything."

"I need to be more confident," Violet admitted. "I do know James loves me, and I need to believe in that. I hope when I tell him, his love for me will make everything all right."

"That's the spirit, Violet." Esmé danced to the door when she heard a tap on it.

Olive waltzed in with two maids behind her. They were laden down under piles of silk. "Place them on the bed," Olive urged. "Thank you both."

Esmé turned away so as not to embarrass anyone while Olive sent the two on their way with a tip.

The pile of silk on the bed overflowed and Esmé noticed Violet looked mesmerized with the white silk and lace dress. Esmé gaze kept going back to the other, which had a *lot* of material to it. The color reminded her of vanilla ice cream.

"I see you both have picked your dresses without me," Olive gushed. "Violet you must try the white on right now!"

"Oh, but...I don't know about this." She bit her lip, unsure.

"You will look so beautiful in the white dress, Violet. Please try it on before you make a decision." Esmé chuckled. "Although, I think if Olive has her way you'll be wearing that dress."

"Esmé and I will sort the dress out so it is ready for you. Go and take that dress off." Olive turned to Violet. "Hurry, I'm so excited."

Violet turned and only briefly hesitated before she took off into the dressing room.

"She's so young," Olive commented, picking the white lace dress up. "But, she's so in love and so is James, and that is all that matters." She smiled. "I'd hoped you would select the other dress. It was made for you."

"It looks beautiful." Esmé glanced at the beautiful vanilla fabric again.

With eyes that twinkled, she said, "It's more daring than anything I've seen before, which is why I couldn't resist it." She leaned closer and whispered, "I bought a new gown in pale pink which is also more daring. Apparently, it's new fashion that will reach America soon. Matthew hasn't seen me in it yet." She blushed. "If I wasn't already pregnant, I would be after wearing that dress."

Esmé blinked and started laughing. "I'm curious now."

"Hmm, what do you think of Violet's choice?" Olive held up the beautiful dress.

"It's plain and simple, so very pretty. This is perfect for Violet." Bending, Esmé lifted the hem and the dress was soft to the touch with layers of the finest silk. "I can't wait to see her in this."

"I'm afraid to touch such beauty," Violet admitted, coming out of the dressing room in her under things. She looked self-conscious so Esmé quickly pulled her toward where they stood and helped Olive get the dress over Violet's head.

"It fits as well." Olive continued fastening the delicate buttons up the back.

Esmé watched Olive, and asked, "Olive, what did Matthew mean about you having a convenient friend? I don't mean to pry but it's been on my mind."

Olive sighed and looked sad, brushing a strand of blonde hair over her ear. "I have a problem keeping my mouth shut. I'm all for manners, but if I don't agree with something then I will say so. I've lost friends because of it, and now I only see them when I can help them with something."

"The lady you bought the dresses for. She's one of them?"

Olive nodded her head as she turned Violet to the mirror. "You look like a princess, Violet."

She really did look like a princess! The cut of the dress was perfect for the girl and the color brought out the warmth of her skin. Esmé eyed up the vanilla mountain of silk. "My turn," she said, turning to the dressing room.

She'd let Olive carry on for now but, when they were in New York together,

Esmé was determined to make sure Olive only had genuine friends.

Esmé had been known for speaking her mind a time or two, and she'd have no problem in doing so when she reached New York, even if it was 1912.

"What is taking you so long?" Violet shouted. "You never take this long to dress."

Rolling her eyes, Esmé stepped into the room and gasped when she saw herself in the mirror. The dress was low on the chest and back, fitted at the waist with yards and yards of material flowing from the waist downwards.

"I knew this one was for you as soon as I looked through the dresses this morning." Olive moved closer. "Why did you take your corset off?" Olive frowned.

Violet giggled and grinned. "I told you ladies *always* wear a corset."

Olive looked between the two of them, so Esmé volunteered, "The thought of wearing one causes me pain, so there is no way I am wearing one. They scare me."

"You're serious?" Olive questioned, dubious.

"Yes." Esmé smoothed her hand over her torso while Olive did up the ribbons. It was so beautiful, and she was right about it being low in the front and back. She'd have to find something else to wear under the dress because her chemise was showing.

"Turn to the side," Olive asked of her. "Stay, just like that." She grabbed hold of the material at the back of the dress and pulled it out toward the floor. "There is so much material to the back of the dress, it's like a train."

Standing back, Olive admired her handiwork. "Esmé, you look stunning." She grinned. "I can't wait to see Luke's face when he sees you." She turned to Violet. "James is going to pass out when he sees you." She dabbed at her eyes and gave Violet and Esmé a hug. "I'm gaining two sisters tomorrow. It makes me so happy."

Esmé watched the other woman. Fighting her own tears, she wanted to squeeze Olive tightly. If history repeated itself, Olive wouldn't survive the sinking. She'd die with her husband and their unborn child.

Her tears trickled down her cheeks and, when Olive and Violet gasped, she let them believe they were tears of emotion over the dress. Not because it broke her heart at the very real possibility Olive would die in the sinking. What would become of Violet and James?

4:00pm

"Do you know that boy?" Luke asked, as he pointed to John, while they walked along the promenade. "I've seen him around a few times, watching us, but he never moves closer."

Esmé gave John a nervous glance before plastering a smile to her face. "It's John. He helped me find my stateroom once we'd set sail from Southampton. I'd gotten lost and somewhat disorientated. He was really very kind."

"Well, I think he has his eye on my lady."

If only it was that simple.

"Oh, stop!" Esmé squeezed Luke's arm.

"I'm sure he has a girl back home, if not on this ship." They moved over to the side of the ship, and Esmé leaned over, watching the ship crash through the waves. "I never thought I'd be on board such a fine ship, or that I would meet the man of my dreams."

Luke moved behind her, shielding her from behind as his hands landed on her hips. He whispered in her ear, "You've very quickly becoming everything to me, Esmé. I can't wait to make you my wife tomorrow. You'll be the loveliest bride." He kissed her cheek. "I'll be telling you that many times tomorrow."

She gave a secretive smile. "When you see me tomorrow in the dress Olive has chosen for me, you won't be able to talk because I'll leave you breathless." She spoke cheekily and with confidence.

His hand slipped around her midriff and he pulled her against him. "You leave me breathless all the time." His lips trailed a blaze of fire along her neck when he nuzzled her hair out of the way. "I love you, Esmé."

She would never get tired of hearing

those words, and she prayed with all her heart they survived the sinking together. Luke did, and she wanted to change her own history. She never wanted to go back to 1987, regardless of what she knew about the First World War, the depression, and all the rest. Her life was tangled with that of Luke's and she would do anything to keep it.

"Why have you become so pensive? Have I frightened you?" Luke asked, his voice heavy with concern.

Esmé took his hands in hers, intertwining their fingers. She turned her head and glanced over her shoulder. "I'm thinking about how much I want to spend the rest of my life with you. I want to see New York through your eyes. I want to take afternoon tea at The St. Regis with Olive and Violet. I want to dine with you at Delmonico's." She turned in his arms and shivered when his hands landed on her bottom before he quickly moved them to her hips. "I want so much with you Luke."

"You know about Delmonico's?" he asked. "It's one of my favorite restaurants."

"I didn't know that, but Delmonico's has been in New York since the 1800s." She grinned. "Word travels."

"It does." He shook his head. "You make me believe that anything is possible."

"Anything is possible," she whispered. "As long as we're together."

"Can I take your photograph?" a voice interrupted.

Luke grinned. "As long as you let me purchase the image."

"You can, Sir." The man set his equipment up.

Luke placed his arm around her, and the image captured was of Esmé's upturned face staring at the man she loved.

The photographer discretely disappeared.

Luke kissed her forehead, and asked, "Do you want to move inside, and join the others?"

"I think I'd rather push two deck chairs together, and sit out here with you." Taking his hand, Esmé led him over and did exactly what she'd suggested. She grabbed two of the thick brown blankets and wrapped one around her shoulders, and the other over her legs. Luke tugged one over his legs too.

"You like the outdoors?" he observed, glancing out across the ocean.

"I do." She turned on her side to face him. "What do you usually do to relax?"

"Read. Whatever I can get my hands on. The paper I will read over breakfast, and then after dinner, I'll read a few chapters of a book; Thomas Hardy and Yeats, to name a few."

"Ah, poetry as well. I read Yeats a while ago." Esmé smiled. "I'm afraid it went in one ear and out the other." She wrinkled her nose and Luke laughed.

"So, what do you like to read?" He smirked.

"Why the laugh, Mr. Carlisle?" Esmé poked him in the stomach.

He chuckled. "Tell me?"

She rolled her eyes, as she went through the list of her favorite authors. She couldn't think of anyone who was published...or even born...before 1912. "Bronte," she suggested and hoped that he hadn't actually read them. For herself, she hadn't read them. They'd never appealed to her. In her own time she'd preferred Robert Crais, Sydney Sheldon, Tom Clancy, and Stephen King.

"Olive enjoys reading the Bronte's. So does my mother." He caressed down her cheek. "What else do you like other than books, my beautiful fiancée?"

"Hmm," she moved closer until his arms wrapped around her body, and he snuggled her against his side, "I love strong coffee, dessert I could eat at every meal."

He laughed, and teased, "I may have noticed that one," before he gave her a long kiss on her forehead.

"I love to dance when I'm in your arms," she continued. "Most of all, I think you've become my new addiction." She became serious and tipped her face to his. "You're all I can think about, Luke. It scares me at how quickly you've become my world."

"Oh, Esmé," he breathed a kiss across her cheek before he tucked her face into the curve of his neck, "you humble me. From the moment we met, our connection was strong and pulsing with life. We'd barely said two words before I kissed you."

She smiled against his neck, remembering. "Our lives are going to change tomorrow," she started nervously, "and I need you to know I love you. I love you so much and I will through eternity and beyond."

She felt him still against her, and she knew she had probably gone too far, but she had to get those words out. It was important to her that he knew just how much she loved him. She really wasn't sure if she'd survive much longer than her wedding day.

"I'm not going to be anywhere else, except by your side, Esmé." He kissed the top of her head. "I promise."

She hoped he'd be able to tell her the same thing on April 16th.

11:20pm

A knock on her stateroom door brought Esmé out of a deep sleep. She felt disorientated, but another knock had her dashing from the bed and grabbing her robe from the chair.

"Who is it?" she whispered.

"John."

Startled, she started to open the door when John quickly slipped through, closing the door behind him. "I can't be seen."

"What's wrong?"

"The fire is out." He walked to her balcony and looked out into the dark night. "I don't know what to do. I can't tell anyone but watching the disaster time and again is tiring. I'm not sure how many more times I can do it."

"There must be a trigger, or a reason why you keep reappearing in the same time."

"No matter what I do to make sure I'm not in the same place as the previous time when the Titanic sinks, I always end up back on the ship in Southampton."

Esmé fidgeted with the belt of her robe. "I've been thinking. What if we do something to slow the ship down? Break the timeline, as we know it? That might even help you."

John stared at her as though he hadn't heard her correctly.

"Think about it, John. We wouldn't have told anyone." She sat on the chair in the room.

"I don't know enough about the workings of the ship to stop her from moving," he slowly admitted.

"What about causing the anchor to drop as we get closer. It would take them time to haul it back up."

John shook his head. "Not sure that would work. It takes a good few men to work the anchor." John grumbled, heading for the door. "We'd still be messing with history." With his hand on the doorknob, he said over his shoulder, "I'll think of something…I can't be on this ship again."

"Hmm." Esmé sighed.

He slipped out as quickly as he'd slipped into her room, leaving Esmé restless.

CHAPTER 16
APRIL 14TH 1912

7:20am

Esmé woke after tossing and turning all night. Her heart raced with a huge sense of loss and, if John was to be believed, there was nothing she could do about the pending disaster. She had to believe him because he *knew* more that she possibly could.

How was she going to go through today, knowing what would become of the ship during the early hours of the following morning? Or would John come up with a way to prevent it?

"Rise and shine." Violet burst into Esmé's room. "It's our wedding day."

At that moment, Esmé knew she would get through the day because she had to. She was marrying the man she loved, and no matter what happened next, he'd be her husband.

She had to focus on the present. She'd worry about the future later. "Why aren't you jumping for joy and bursting with excitement?"

"I will be later. I had a bad night's sleep."

"Too excited I suspect," Violet mumbled. "I was going to tell James today about being a maid, but I blurted it out last night." She grinned and sat beside Esmé on the bed. "Turns out he'd suspected as such. He said he didn't care how I'd boarded the ship, as long as I disembarked as his wife."

"I'm delighted for you." Esmé squeezed the girl's arm. "And now that I'm more awake, I'm feeling refreshed and ready for anything." She stretched and flung the covers off. "I'm skipping church this morning because I want to move all my things into Luke's room. We'll get fresh linen in here. James and yourself can have this room."

"Oh! You can't do that," Violet said, appalled.

"Violet, I happen to know that James has a single room, which means you both will be more comfortable in here with this nice big bed," Esmé smiled and turned away while Violet got her blush under control.

"But..."

"No buts, Violet." Esmé turned back and gently took Violet's hands into hers, pulling her to the bed. "I don't want to embarrass you, but do you know about, um, what to expect on your wedding night?"

Violet went the color of the strawberries they'd eaten the day before, and gently shook her head.

"Don't be afraid or embarrassed. Just enjoy his touch. He'll want to please you, just like you'll want to please him."

"It's supposed to hurt," Violet said.

"Not always. Sometimes, there is a bit of discomfort, but after the first time it won't hurt. It's one way for two people to share their love for each other. It's meant to be beautiful." Esmé smiled softly and kissed Violet on the cheek. "Now." She jumped up. "No more talk about refusing this room. Think of it as a wedding gift if you wish. However, I plan on sharing Luke's room from this point forward."

Esmé quickly disappeared into the dressing room, closing the door behind her before Violet could see the heartbreak on her face.

Her legs gave out as she settled onto the floor, looking around the small room. It would be another seventy-three years before the ship would be seen again.

Why hadn't she learned more about the Titanic once she'd met Luke? She should have. Maybe she'd have discovered a lifeboat that took men as well as women and children. Perhaps she'd have discovered whether or not she'd survived. So many thoughts, and although she couldn't say anything, she could prepare everyone later that evening. Make sure the six of them got off the ship before it was too late.

As far as she knew, helping once the disaster had struck wasn't against anyone's rules. She'd be helping.

Holding onto the dresser, she pulled herself up and glanced at herself in the mirror. She was pale. Too pale for someone whose wedding day it was.

If she didn't pull herself together, Luke would know there was something wrong, She might even think she'd changed her mind about marrying him. That couldn't happen.

Her stomach in knots, Esmé quickly dressed and slipped her feet into a pair of boots. The items on the dressing table were swiped off and placed into a box.

"Violet, can you help me get the clothes, please?" Esmé grabbed a handful of dresses and moved to drop them onto the bed. "We need to sort them out. Split them. You need to have your own things." She spun around. "We'll do that now. Everything I'm giving you can stay in the closet, and the things I'm taking into Luke's room can go on the bed for now. We have a few hours before the wedding."

"I could do with eating something," Violet confessed, her hand pressed on her stomach.

"I'd forgotten about breakfast. Let's get something quick, and then we can come back and finish sorting out before we have to dress."

"That's a good idea." Violet grinned and was the first to the door. "Um, don't you think you should brush your hair first?"

Esmé reached up and realized she'd forgone everything in her rush to get into Luke's room. "Oh. One minute."

She ran back into the dressing room, quickly brushed her hair and applied some moisturizer. At least she had a bit of color now because the moisturizer was tinted.

"I'm ready." She twirled and curtsied in front of Violet. "Let's go and eat."

She slid her arm through Violets and led the girl to the dinning saloon. Her mind wouldn't settle, it refused to let her forget the events that were coming that evening.

It made her wonder why she was going ahead with switching staterooms, but she knew she had to go through with the motions as though she didn't know the future. In a way, she wished she didn't.

"Good morning, Miss."

Her eyes snapped to the left, finding John standing in the hallway.

"Morning, John. This is my friend Violet."

He tipped his head to her, but his eyes focused on Esmé. "You can help, but not interfere." He held her gaze and Esmé nodded to let him know she'd gotten his message.

She pulled Violet with her into breakfast.

"What did he mean?" Violet asked her brows pulled tight.

Esmé glanced behind them but he'd gone. When she turned back to Violet, she told her, "I asked him something yesterday, but he got called away before he could answer." Esmé smiled and patted Violet's hand. "I assure you, everything is fine."

"Hmm," Violet mumbled, selecting egg and toast for breakfast.

With a heavy sigh, Esmé followed, hoping her appetite would come back. It was difficult—knowing more than half of the people in the room with them wouldn't be alive come morning.

3:00pm

Esmé felt as though her heart would pound right out of her chest while she waited outside of the room with Matthew. He'd been chosen to give her away since there was no one else. "You both look beautiful," Matthew said as they walked up. Violet's cheeks flushed at the compliment. "There's no need to be nervous. My brother loves you." He turned to Violet. "As does James." He chuckled. "The Titanic should be renamed the Love Boat." He straightened his dinner jacket.

Startled, Esmé glanced at him and finally had her nerves settle. "I'm excited to be marrying him. I'm just...nervous." She wasn't nervous about what was to come, she was terrified, but she couldn't exactly announce that. She actually wanted to shout it from the highest point on the ship.

"They're ready for you," the ships Purser informed.

Esmé placed her hand on her stomach and took a deep inhale. A calmness she hadn't felt all morning settled over her, and as Matthew offered his arm to Violet, and the three of them walked through the doors.

The number of passengers in attendance surprised her, but the moment her eyes landed on Luke, he was all she saw. He took her breath away, standing tall and handsome in his dinner suit that was fitted to his large frame perfectly. His hair was neatly brushed back, and the look on his face was one she would never forget for as long as she'd live.

They may have only met a few days ago, but their feelings were very real, and she knew what they had would last beyond anything else.

The captain cleared his throat to get the attention of everyone in the room. His words mingled together as Esmé lost her focus when she witnessed the tender love in Luke's gaze. She couldn't say how long it took, she just knew that the moment the captain pronounced them man and wife, her love for Luke was beyond anything she'd experienced before.

Passengers cheered as Luke pulled her into his arms for a rather tame kiss. When he moved away, brushing his lips softly across Esmé's, he whispered, "Hello, Mrs. Carlisle."

Esmé beamed a smile. "Hello, my husband."

Luke's hand trembled as he gently caressed her cheek before they turned to James and Violet. They'd been married alongside them, and Esmé felt guilty for not paying them any attention...until now, as she caught the other woman up in her arms.

"Congratulations," the pair exchanged hugs while James and Luke shook hands with each other, the captain, and purser.

Luke took her hand and her heart felt full. The temptation to pinch herself made her fingers twitch. Her wedding day was April 14th, 1912. She was born in 1962, although on the wedding license, she'd signed it 1886 because her birthday was in October. She just had to keep the date in her mind—it was almost too much to keep straight.

Passengers offered good wishes and, as Luke led her through them, she wondered what condition they'd all be in later. Providing she was one of the lucky ones and Luke didn't lose her to the ocean. How many of the faces smiling at them would she see on the Carpathia? Not many.

She tried to keep the smile on her face but it was becoming difficult, and forced. She was happy. She was happier than she could ever remember being. She had just married her soul mate. The man she'd first met in the future, and the man who completed her in the past. It was hard to comprehend, and something told her not to even try to work it all out.

"Are you feeling all right, Esmé? You've gone pale." Luke touched her cheeks with his cool fingers.

Esmé reached up and wrapped a small hand around his wrist. "I am well, and so happy to be your wife." She smiled, and it reached her eyes, a real smile for her very real husband. "I love you," she whispered, tilting her face up to his for a leisurely kiss.

"The captain has invited us to eat dinner at his table this evening," Violet gushed. "It will be fun."

Esmé hid her amusement from Violet, and laughed at the look on James's face. She thought he had other ideas for the rest of the day, just like she had with Luke.

"I'm sure we can make dinner." Luke pulled a pocket watch out of his jacket. "There is around four hours before dinner." He grinned. "I suggest we go our separate ways until then."

"What a good idea," James agreed.

After a group photograph, Esmé slipped her hand into Luke's and, with a gentle tug, had him moving with her. She snuggled against his arm. "I'm so happy right now, Luke."

"I have the most beautiful bride in the world on my arm, I couldn't be any happier." He wrapped an arm around her shoulders. "Your clothes look really good hanging in the closet with mine."

She grinned. "I knew they would. I just

hope James and Violet don't feel uncomfortable using my stateroom. It's not as though I need it now."

"Don't worry. I've already spoken to James about it, and he's really fine with moving rooms. He knows that his room, although a stateroom, isn't big enough for the two of them." He placed a sweet kiss on her cheek. "I'm just looking forward to not having to part from you in the evenings. I missed you when we'd part company."

"No more." Esmé sighed and followed Luke into his room.

CHAPTER 17

1987

"I can't believe Violet and Luke spent a few years together in the same nursing home."

"Up until a few weeks ago, you had no real interest in the Titanic." Jake shrugged. "Maybe you'll recognize her and remember her once we see her."

"Maybe." Sienna hesitated on the last step that would take her inside. "I'm nervous, Jake. What if she tells us that Esmé died during the sinking. I think it would break my heart."

"The not knowing is killing me," he admitted. "Come on, let's go and find out." He opened the door and ushered her inside to the large reception desk.

"Who are you here to see?" asked the nurse, looking half asleep.

"Violet Calder," Jake said, pulling the sign in book toward him to add their names while Sienna looked around in curiosity.

She could see a homey common area in the room beyond the reception with couches and chairs. The same grumpy nurse led them through a wide hallway conducive to wheelchairs. On the wall, facing the door they'd come through, was a special events board for the home, offering movie nights and bingo. There wasn't much in decorations until they walked further into the home.

A huge fish tank sat to one end of the cafeteria, the tables covered with silk flower arrangements. The noise from the TV room could be heard out in the hallway, but they walked past for a few feet, where they stopped.

"She's in there. Been expecting you." The nurse walked off, leaving them to look at each other.

"What if…"

"Shush." Jake covered her mouth. "There

are no what ifs okay? We are going to go in there and have a proper conversation with her."

Sienna held his gaze and knew he was right. "I can do this."

"We can do this," Jake muttered as he pushed the door open.

The room was much larger than Sienna had expected, with a bay window overlooking the front pond.

A lovely Victorian dressing table sat beside the chair where Violet waited for them, watching the door. At a quick glance, Sienna's eyes widened when she spotted the open door of the closet. She blinked a few times and found herself moving closer. At the door, she hesitated.

"You can look," Violet offered. "They're all mine from years gone by."

Very carefully Sienna reached forward and pulled out a royal blue dress that was down to the floor. The material felt soft to the touch and had Sienna turning to Violet. "This is beautiful." She shook her head and placed it back inside the closet, glancing at the others.

"I think my mind is stuck in the past," Violet offered.

Sienna moved closer and scanned the black and white photographs in beautiful frames covering the dresser, and that's all Sienna saw—her attention completely captivated.

"You like my collection?" Violet asked, her stare unmoving.

Sienna wet her lips with the tip of her tongue. "I do. Very much so."

Violet didn't smile but moved her gaze to the two chairs that had been placed around where she sat. Jake urged Sienna into one and then sat beside her.

"Why are you here?"

Sienna glanced at Jake and winced, except he offered her an encouraging smile, and said, "Have you met Luke Carlisle's caregiver, Sienna?"

The old lady snapped her eyes to Sienna and stared as though she willed her to burst into flames. After a few minutes, she finally smiled. "You want to know about Luke?"

"That's why we're here," Sienna informed her, leaning forward. "We wanted to know anything you can tell us about him, about his time on the Titanic and, afterwards, his life in New York. What happened to him on board that ship?"

For a while, Violet sat in silence, a million thoughts crossing her face as they watched her. Tears sprung in her old eyes. Her face was wrinkled with age, but she looked as though she didn't miss anything. Her dress was black, and styled in a similar way as the others in the closet. She dressed as though she was still on the ship.

Sienna met Violet's gaze, and admitted to the elderly lady with a head full of silver hair, "Before Luke died, he became obsessed with a friend of Jake's." She glanced briefly at him, and then focused back on Violet. "He kept telling her to, and I quote, 'find me in the past', which was a strange thing to say. He gave her a locket that refused to open."

"Until the night she wore the dress Luke had given her. It opened, right before she disappeared," Jake added.

They certainly had Violet's attention

now. "Disappeared?" She frowned, but a knowing look flashed across her face.

"The woman we are trying to find information on is named Esmé Rogers." Jake took Sienna's hand the moment he said Esmé's name.

The woman gasped and stilled, clutching a hand to her chest. When she appeared to be struggling for breath, Sienna jumped up to help her.

Violet waved her off. "I'm fine. It was a shock hearing her name after all these years."

"You knew her?"

Violet turned her head toward the photographs on her dresser, and whispered, "She gave me the life I've lived all these years with the man I fell in love with on the Titanic. I'm ready to join him now. I have been since the day he died without me."

Sienna had to blink away tears, and Jake was in the same position.

"I boarded the ship as Esmé's maid. Within an hour of knowing her, she announced we were the best of friends. I was never a maid again." She sighed and dipped her head. "Can you pass me the large wedding photograph please?"

"Yeah, sure." Jake found the one Violet meant and stood staring at the photograph before he lifted his gaze and met Sienna's. "Esmé and Luke are on here. They married on the Titanic?" He watched Violet who stared at the photograph in his hands.

"A double wedding. April 14th, 1912." Violet smiled, lost in the past. "Esmé was so in love with Luke, and he loved her with every breath in his body. When she disappeared without a trace, he changed. He wouldn't talk about her. He closed himself off from everyone."

"When did she disappear?" Sienna asked the question they wanted to know the answer to the most.

Violet asked a question of her own, "How did Luke find her?"

"It's a crazy story, if you have time?"

She laughed. "I haven't walked in a few years young man, so I don't think I'm going anywhere."

CHAPTER 18
APRIL 14TH, 1912

4:00pm

The moment they were behind the closed door of their stateroom, Luke encircled her, one large hand on her stomach. The pulse in Esmé's neck throbbed with excitement and her heart raced, wanting and needing her handsome husband.

"I'm nervous," he admitted, burying his face against her neck. "I shouldn't be admitting that to you."

"Oh Luke! If you can't admit it to me, then who can you admit it to?" Esmé turned. She wound her arms inside his jacket, around his back, and delighted when he shuddered in response. "I'm nervous too, but it makes me feel more confident knowing that you're nervous."

"I haven't done this before." Luke offered a wry smile.

She blinked up at him. "You haven't?"

He laughed, embarrassed. "I've never had an interest in a loveless coupling."

Esmé was thrilled at his declaration, and pressed her soft curves into the hard contours of his strong body. "I'm glad."

"I want to be gentle with you," he confessed, his hands trembling as his fingers caressed over her neck and shoulders.

The mere touch of his hand sent a warming shiver through her as she gasped. "I love having your hands on me, but I want them on more of me." She stepped away from his touch and slowly unfastened the ribbon at the front of the dress. "I don't want to disappoint you," she confessed, holding his gaze.

"You could never disappoint me, Esmé. My love for you is unconditional. I love you now, and I'll love you when you are round

COME BACK TO ME

with my child. My love will never stop."
While he talked, he'd removed the top part
of his clothing, his arousal blatantly obvious
when her eyes moved downwards in a
caress.

Esmé let the cream-colored dress pool
around her feet. The only sound in the
room was the harsh breathing coming from
Luke, as she stood nude before him.

"So beautiful," he whispered, quickly removing the remainder of his clothing. "I've
never seen anyone as beautiful as you are
right now, and you're all mine."

"Yes, I am." Her breasts heaved when he
slowly moved toward her.

His fingers roamed intimately over her
breasts, the rosy peaks growing to pebble
hardness at the gentle touch. Taking her
hand, he hesitantly guided it to himself
and she felt the smooth skin over his
hardness.

Luke gasped and trembled at her touch,
which gave her a heady sensation. She lifted
her other hand and thread her fingers
through the hair on his chest. His whole
body shuddered seconds before she found

herself crushed against his chest—his mouth pressed to hers.

The feel of his chest rubbing against her sensitive breasts caused her to squirm in his arms. She wanted and needed more and, by the urgency of his touch, so did he.

Their need grew as Luke took three strides toward the large bed, and laid her down beneath him. He held her gaze and, very slowly, moved lower—fondling one small globe, its pink nipple marble hard. He kissed the other taut nipple, rousing a melting sweetness within her. His tongue seared a path down her ribs to her stomach and further down, sending currents of desire through her.

He took her hands, encouraging them to explore as she caressed the length of his back when he moved over her.

"So beautiful, Esmé," he whispered as he gathered her against his warm pulsing body. She instinctively arched toward him, welcoming him into her body. His hardness electrified her with a pleasure that was pure and explosive.

Her body melted against his. Her world

was filled with him. Her Luke. Her husband. Together, they found the tempo that bound their bodies together in exquisite harmony.

A moan of ecstasy slipped through her lips and the feel of his rough skin against hers assaulted her senses. Love flowed inside her like warm honey as she was hurtled beyond the point of return, crying out for release.

They soared higher and higher until they reached the peak of delight, and they both exploded in a downpour of fiery sensations. Waves of ecstasy throbbed through her before contentment and peace flowed between them.

Luke sighed in pleasant exhaustion as Esmé snuggled against him, their legs intertwined while she was conscious of where his warm flesh pressed against her.

"That was…"

"Beautiful," Esmé finished, her head resting on his chest while her fingers played with his chest hair.

"I want to spend the rest of our time, on board this ship, just like this," Luke whispered into her hair. "I don't want real life to intrude until we have to disembark."

Esmé wiggled higher and buried her face into the curve of his neck, knowing she had to have Luke dressed in warm clothing later this evening. She may not be able to tell him what would happen within mere hours, but she could prepare him and their friends and family.

"You've gone quiet," he observed, hesitant.

To take his mind off her distraction, she distracted him instead, and breathed a kiss against his neck. "I didn't sleep well last night because I was excited for today. I'm pleasantly tired and don't want to move from your arms."

"At least we are in agreement about that." He wrapped a curl around his finger and tugged. "I could leave, excuse us for not joining the others at dinner, and then bring back some food?"

She smiled. "I'd like," she kissed his jaw, "to eat a wedding dinner with Violet, James, your brother and his wife." She blushed slightly. "Besides, when your mother asks what we did on our wedding day, I'd rather have something to tell her that isn't going to make us blush."

He chuckled. "Yeah, that would be a tricky one, although I'm sure my mother would never ask the question, but it would be nice to eat with everyone, I guess."

Tickling him on the side, he wiggled and laughed, while Esmé chuckled. "You could sound more enthusiastic."

"I'm very enthusiastic," he growled, rolling her to her back before he slipped inside the warmth of her body, "for you."

CHAPTER 19

1987

Violet sat in silence and stared at Sienna and Jake. They'd retold the story from Esmé's first meeting with Luke, to the night she'd disappeared in front of Jake. It was an incredulous story, and Sienna knew they sounded crazy but she needed Violet to believe them.

"That explains a lot," Violet finally whispered, her hands trembling. "She was bothered about something and didn't know how to tell Luke. Eventually, they agreed to talk about what troubled her once they arrived in New York." She held Sienna's gaze. "She would have known what happened to the

Titanic beforehand if she came from this year?"

"She did." Jake sat forward. "I take it she never said anything?"

Violet slowly shook her head. "Not one word, except..." her gaze misted over and, for ten minutes, Violet was lost to the past. "I don't understand how it's possible to travel through time, but, for what happened later, I don't think I would believe you."

"What happened?" Sienna asked, eager.

Violet ignored her question. "That evening," she whispered, "after our wedding, and dinner at the captain's table, she asked us to meet her on deck at eleven-thirty. She told us to wear our warmest clothing; hat, gloves, anything to keep us warm." She wiped tears from her eyes. "We weren't too keen and neither was Luke because it was their wedding night after all."

She smiled softly, and then her eyes filled with anguish. "When the Titanic hit the iceberg, we were on deck. You could feel the impact as it vibrated throughout the ship."

"So she never told anyone what was going to happen?"

"Not that I'm aware of. She didn't even tell us, just made sure we were dressed for the cold weather. A while later, she caused an argument at a life boat." She sighed. "I think I need to rest now." She looked at her photographs, and added, "If you'd both like to come back tomorrow, I'll tell you more, and what happened on board the Carpathia."

Jake laughed and Sienna looked surprised while Violet gave them a sly smile, knowing that she'd bated the hook. They'd be back.

"Thank you for talking to us," Sienna said, getting to her feet.

"We appreciate your time." Jake took hold of Sienna's hand.

"I didn't know you knew Luke and Esmé when you'd arranged to come see me."

Jake nodded, and tugged Sienna out of the room.

They stayed silent until they had driven a few miles away from the home, and then

Sienna asked, "Do you think Esmé made it to the Carpathia?"

Sighing heavily, Jake replied, "I think she did. Violet didn't indicate anything else, and I think she would have said if she'd been lost on the Titanic. As far as I'm aware, nothing happened on the Carpathia that made it into the history books." He tapped the steering wheel. "Maybe we should head toward the library and have a look through the newspaper articles from then; see if anything shows up."

"I'd rather go home and eat," Sienna said quietly, it had been a long day and she was ready to go home. "Besides, whatever happened, we'll find out about it tomorrow. I hope at least."

"Violet knew how to get us back to visit with her." Jake chuckled. "Do you think she's lonely? We don't really know anything about her life."

Sienna settled with her head against the seat and admired Jake in profile. He needed a shave, although she found she liked him like this—denim and plaid—handsome in a rugged sort of way. She preferred him this way instead of in his suits because he was much more approachable.

"A dime for your thoughts?" he asked, frowning.

When they got stuck behind a delivery truck, she reached out and rubbed gently along his forehead. "I'm not thinking anything that is worth that frown." She smiled softly, meeting his gaze.

Jake slowly moved closer, and then his lips softly brushed hers as he spoke, "I think too hard sometimes." His lips pressed against hers, devouring its softness.

A loud horn blasted behind their car, parting them, her lips were still warm and moist from his kiss as his eyes lingered on her face. Jake swallowed hard before he pulled back into traffic. "Will you let me take you to dinner?" She quickly sent him a smile. "And we'll talk about everything except Esmé and the Titanic."

"You have a deal." Sienna beamed, excited that Esmé wasn't the only one finding happiness.

CHAPTER 20
APRIL 14TH, 1912

7:30pm

The smile on Esmé's face matched the blush on Violet's when their gazes met. Violet laughed, hugging James's side.

"Your friend is happy," Luke whispered into Esmé's ear with a chuckle. His lips brushed a kiss along her neck before he straightened, and winked. "I know the feeling," he mumbled as he turned and greeted his brother.

"This is exciting," Olive gushed, pulling Esmé into an embrace. "Matthew's mother is going to be beside herself when we arrive home. I'm giving her another grandchild to dote on and Luke has given her a new daughter."

Esmé felt as though her smile was frozen in place. She longed for all the talk of tomorrow but she knew what tonight would offer to many of the people in the room. And she wanted to save all of them. She was heartsick. Why had she appeared on the Titanic, when she wasn't able to change the course of events? Surely there had to be a reason? The not knowing frustrated her.

"I think they're ready for us in the saloon," Matthew commented, nodding in the direction of the waving purser.

"Why did we agree to this?" Luke mumbled.

Esmé smiled up at him with a twinkle in her eyes. "Because we thought it would be a lovely way to remember our wedding day."

"I'll remember our wedding day as long as I live." Luke quickly kissed her cheek and hovered. "I want to capture your lips with mine, but I think I'd cause too much trouble if I did that here."

Esmé licked her lips in thought while

she stared into his eyes. "I'm not sure I'd want you to stop."

Luke made a noise at the back of his throat before he quickly took Esmé by the arm and marched her into the dining saloon, much to her amusement. "You are incorrigible, Mr. Carlisle."

He beamed a smile. "You shouldn't be so enchanting, Mrs. Carlisle."

"I see the newlyweds are on time," the captain stated. "Please sit."

The first thing Esmé noted was their wedding photograph, which brought tears to her eyes. Luke kissed her cheek and, after a closer look, pocketed it. "I won't ever lose this, or forget how mesmerizing you looked in your wedding gown."

"And I won't forget how handsome my husband was in his tuxedo."

Luke held her gaze and Esmé blushed at the intensity in his gaze.

He squeezed her hand, bringing their attention to the beautifully set table. A small cake sat in front of each place setting. As she glanced around the table, they alternated with Luke and her initials, and Violet and James's.

"Ah, you've spotted tonight's treat! I instructed Chief Baker to come up with something special, and he hasn't let me down."

"They're beautiful," Esmé sighed, smiling when she overheard Violet asking James what he thought they were.

"Cake," the captain added, his lips twitching. "And here are our other guests."

Esmé glanced over her shoulder and smiled at the approaching couple. She had no idea who they were, but she'd seen them around the ship and in the saloon a few times.

The woman, who the captain introduced as Scarlett Young, was older than Esmé. Her beautiful blue silk dress covered with silver beads looked amazing, and Esmé found she couldn't move her eyes away. "Your dress is beautiful," she whispered, finally raising her gaze to meet Scarlett's.

"Thank you." Scarlett smiled. "My sister and I love to sew. I've discovered our creations always hold the attention of others.

I'll only wear our clothing now. This is one of mine."

"You're very talented," Esmé commented, turning to Luke when he urged her into a seat.

"My wife dazzles," Edward, her husband added with a robust smile. "I believe congratulations are in order?" he announced.

Scarlett raised her glass. "Yes, I think we should toast the newlyweds."

"To the newlyweds," the captain toasted.

A few minutes later, Esmé offered, "Violet is interested in the design business." She grinned at Violet, and gave her hand a quick squeeze.

"My wife can do anything her heart desires when we reach New York," James said, gruffly. "Even learning how to make wonderful, eye catching, gowns."

Violet blushed, but Esmé didn't miss the love shining in her fierce gaze for her new husband.

"Thank you," she held his hand.

Luke caught her attention. "Everything all right?" he whispered in Esmé's ear, sending shards of pleasure down her spine.

Her lips skimmed his as she turned to face him. "Everything is perfect."

She caught John trying to get her attention from the entrance of the dining saloon. She figured, by his actions, he wanted her to meet him after she'd eaten.

Even the breath of a kiss Luke had brushed against her cheek couldn't dispel the nerves rapidly growing in her belly.

9:00pm

Luke placed a lingering kiss to her cheek before he disappeared with his brother and James to the smoke room. She hadn't missed the wince he'd given her. He hated the smoke room, so he wouldn't be in there long.

She only half listened to Olive, Violet, and Scarlett, while she excused herself, "I'll only be a minute." Olive and Scarlett smiled and Violet frowned with a glance toward the doorway where John had been before she glanced back to Esmé.

Esmé placed her hand on the younger girl's shoulder. "It's fine."

As she moved between passengers and other tables, her heart raced with hope that John had found a way to at least slow the ship down. When she found him waiting for her, she knew he hadn't come up with anything. His face was downcast and he appeared disheveled.

"Nothing."

He shook his head. "I can't ask anyone because, if they told, I'd be taken away by Master at Arms. It's serious to sabotage a ship," he whispered.

"I know, but you'd be saving lives."

"They don't know what is going to happen, and we can't tell them unless we want to disappear." He waved his arms around, agitated.

Esmé paced in front of him. A quick glance in the dining saloon confirmed that Luke hadn't returned.

She paused. "I can't believe I never thought to ask until now, but do you ever make it onto a lifeboat?"

He slowly shook his head, his eyes

showing fear. "Every time, I go into the water."

Her heart went out to him, so quickly as she noticed Luke appear, she said, "I'm going to get my family to meet on deck at eleven-thirty. You meet us too. We're all going to get off this ship." She turned and headed toward Luke with a smile plastered on her face.

She really hoped John met them on deck, and that she would be successful in getting them all into lifeboats. That was her only option now.

"I wondered where you had disappeared to," Luke commented, wrapping an arm around her shoulders.

"A bit of fresh air." She smiled, her conscience eating away at her.

Scarlett and Edward slipped away, so she turned to the others. "I know this is going to sound crazy, but please don't ask me questions I can't answer."

"What is it, Esmé? You can tell me anything." Luke brushed a curl over her shoulder.

"It's not that, but I will explain, I promise." She bit her lip as she thought of her plan. " For now, I need you to just meet us on deck at eleven-thirty," she hurriedly said. "It's really important. Dress warmly."

They stared at her but nodded in acceptance. "We'll be there," James said.

"I'm curious, so we will join you," Matthew added.

She turned to Luke. "Can we go back to our room?"

"Of course." He offered a wry smile, his hand slipping to her waist.

10:00pm

"I love you," Luke said the minute the door to their stateroom closed. "I am extremely curious, but I trust you to tell me what is going on once we reach New York."

Esmé wrapped her arms around her husband's waist and felt Luke rest his chin on the top of her head. "Thank you. I want to tell you now, but I can't for reasons I can't tell you. I will explain it all, I promise.

I know I'm being cryptic, but it's a huge relief that you trust me."

He kissed the top of her head as he held her tight against his chest. They stayed like that until Luke gently cupped her chin and raised her face to his.

Love was reflected in his gaze as his face lowered to hers, his tongue tracing the soft fullness of her lips, sending shivers of desire racing through her. He raised his mouth from hers, his lips wet—his eyes full of desire. "I love you, Esmé," his words were smothered on her lips.

Esmé slipped her fingers into Luke's hair and held him against her. She shivered when Luke skimmed his hands over her waist and hips, and then he finally unfastened her dress, letting it drop to the floor. "Exquisite," Luke whispered, a tremble to his hands.

Unable to wait any longer, Esmé reached out and quickly helped Luke free himself from the restriction of his clothing. Her body was overtaken with desire and nerves. Before Luke could see her blush with embarrassment, she buried her face against his chest, her arms wrapping around his waist. Her breasts tingled against his hair-roughened chest. Luke gave a loud groan and shuddered in her arms.

"I need you," Esmé confessed. "I need you right now." She tilted her face up to Luke's.

He swallowed hard and laid her gently on the bed. She gasped at the sensation of his body over hers, his penis thick and heavy. His lips brushed her nipples while she lay panting beneath him—her chest heaving. She writhed under him, eager for more.

His fingers burned against her tingling skin as they slid over her silken belly and moved downward, skimming either side of her body to her thighs. One of his hands slipped to her bottom while Esmé wrapped her hand around the warmth of his arousal.

"You feel like silk," Esmé whispered in wonder, grasping him in her hand. "But hard as steel."

Luke groaned, his hand lightly touching her hardened nipples before he dipped his head, capturing one in his mouth. Esmé rose to meet him in a moment of uncontrolled passion. He slipped inside her welcoming heat, a shiver of ecstasy running through them both. Her body melted against him and the world filled with only Luke. Her husband.

His touch was divine ecstasy, and her hands reached for him, caressing the length of his back before massaging the tendons in his neck. Flames of passion burned within them both. His breathing was labored as she felt sweet agony before waves of ecstasy throbbed through her and they shattered into a million glowing stars.

Luke wrapped her into his embrace and rolled them to their sides, his weight crushing her. Contentment and peace flowed between them as Luke picked up a lock of Esmé's hair and caressed it gently between his thumb and finger.

"I love you with everything in me," Esmé whispered, succumbing to the numbed sleep of the satisfied lover.

Unable to settle, Luke moved from the bed and quickly dressed. He poured himself a whiskey and settled into the armchair, his eyes caressing over his wife. He had a sickening feeling that if he closed his eyes, then his beautiful Esmé would disappear. He couldn't live without her.

11:30pm

It was cold on deck as Esmé rubbed her hands together for warmth. Luke covered them with his large hands and blew warm air onto them. "I hadn't realized how cold it was on deck so late at night." Luke paused. "The bed keeps us nice and warm," he whispered for Esmé's ears only.

She blushed slightly before she offered him a dazzling smile.

"Blimey, it's so cold," Violet complained, James's arm around her shoulders.

"You can say that again," Matthew added, glancing at Esmé before a crewman caught his eye. He nodded toward the man. "He probably thinks we are all crazy being out here at this time."

Esmé winced. After all, she knew what

was about to happen, and they didn't. She became uneasy by the second as her dismay grew. An uncertainty crept into Luke's face, as she remained silent, watching him. What could she say? There was nothing that would put them at ease. And in a few minutes, it would be a race against time to get them all safely off the ship. Especially as she knew the captain would order all women and children first.

"Esmé?" Luke questioned.

Her mind was congested with doubts and fear as her eyes met those of her husband. When she tried to speak, her voice wavered, so she snapped her mouth closed.

Luke reached up and caressed her face before resting his forehead against hers. "I trust you."

Before she had chance to respond, John ran up to her.

She quickly turned and met his anxious gaze. "Now." The minute John uttered the word; panicked shouts could be heard.

"What's that all about?" Matthew mumbled, stepping closer to the side of the ship to see what the crew was looking at.

James followed, his hand clasped tightly around Violet's as though he didn't want her anywhere but by his side.

Esmé clasped Luke's hand and slowly looked up, fear knotted inside of her as she caught the first glimpse of the iceberg. It looked over a hundred feet tall, rising up from the ocean.

James, Violet, and Matthew, moved back quickly, their feet thundering on deck along with those of panicked crew. Matthew wrapped Olive up in his arms and held her close against his chest.

There were a handful of passengers close by and they appeared frozen.

Overwhelming fear raced through Esmé as she watched the disaster start to unfold in front of her eyes.

Luke wrapped his arms around her middle from behind and quickly stepped further away from the iceberg.

"We have to get below deck," he shouted.

His words broke through Esmé's fear. "No!" She panicked. "We can't go below deck."

Suddenly chunks of ice landed on the

deck to gasps and cries. The sound of the iceberg cutting into Titanic's hull was something she'd never forget. The loud groan was like a leviathan was rising from the murky depths—the ship screaming in pain and fear. It was terrifying and Esmé wanted to run, she just had nowhere to run to. "It's damaging the ship," James said in disbelief. "Sounds like it's cutting her open."

He doesn't know how accurate that description is.

Esmé turned grief stricken eyes to Luke, whose face had turned white. "You knew this was going to happen?"

Tears trembled on Esmé's eyelids, as she slowly nodded. "I can't say more. I desperately want to, but I can't." The tears slipped down her cheek.

"Esmé?" her name was shouted in a rush, filled with impatience.

She turned within the circle of Luke's arms, having forgotten about John, which didn't sit well on her conscience.

"You know what to do," he said turning away.

Esmé reached out and grabbed his arm. "What do I do?"

John paused. "Find a boat that will take men." He ran off.

"What did he mean?" Olive whispered, confused while she hung tightly to Matthew, her face full of fear.

The other two couples moved closer so she admitted in a voice tight with anxiety, "There are not enough lifeboats for everyone." She inhaled and held Luke's gaze. "The usual rule of women and children first will obviously apply. There will be no boats left for the men." Fear stark and vivid, flittered in her eyes.

Luke forced a smile and caressed her cold cheek with a finger. "I love you." He tugged a loose curl behind her ear. "So much, Esmé." Tears welled in his eyes.

Smothering a sob, she flung herself into his arms. "I will not leave you." Tears clogged her throat. "Do you hear me? We leave together," she cried.

CHAPTER 21
APRIL 15TH, 1912

12:45am

Time passed quickly as the panic and confusion grew. It wasn't long before passengers started to become aware that the ship was doomed.

In a panic, people surrounded the first lifeboat to be loaded, some hesitant, not truly believing getting in the boat was a necessity. Eventually it was slowly lowered—half empty—onto the ocean below. Others grumbled and tried to push through to the next lifeboat.

Esmé wished she didn't know what she

did because she wanted to tell Luke and the others what would happen. There was an ice-cold ball of fear in her belly that she wouldn't be able to save her family, and, most importantly, the man she loved.

"We need to find a lifeboat. Get the women off," Matthew said, a hint of fear in his voice as his gaze searched his wife's face.

Luke tightened his arms around Esmé as a wave of loss suddenly overwhelmed her. Tears stung her eyes as unrelenting as the cold night air. "I'm not leaving this ship unless Luke is with me."

"Esmé," Luke said, softly. He turned her to face him. "I want to know you're safe." He kissed her forehead. "I need you safe."

Reaching up, Esmé cupped Luke's handsome face. "That's what I need for you as well. Please don't ask me to leave without you."

He sighed heavily, and tugged her against his chest.

"I agree with Esmé. We all leave, or, we all stay," Violet stated, her lips quivering.

"No," Matthew disagreed. "Olive is pregnant and needs to get off this boat with or without me."

Olive burst into tears and buried her face against Matthew's chest. Matthew rested his chin on the top of her head with tears on his face.

It was obvious to Esmé that Olive and Matthew needed off the boat first, but how was the biggest dilemma. She had to try and save them, even knowing their fate.

While the orchestra played in the background, Esmé stayed quiet, thinking. She couldn't concentrate because all her thoughts were on the man whose arms held her securely against him.

With a sudden burst of fear, Esmé pulled away from Luke. "Follow me."

Luke grabbed her hand and kept her locked tightly with him while she pushed and shoved her way through the desperate passengers.

Another lifeboat had female passengers and children on board, but it was by no means full as intended.

"Wait!" Esmé shouted.

"Get on, Miss. Hurry!"

Esmé shoved Olive closer. "You need to rescue her. She's pregnant, and her husband has to go with her."

The crewman on the lifeboat shook his head. "No men. Captain's orders."

Esmé had a thought as she glanced at the others in the lifeboat. "Who is going to row once in the water?"

The startled crewman looked around. Esmé continued, "Matthew is stronger than anyone in the boat. He can row you quickly to a safe distance. I promise. You need him."

The crewman nervously glanced around. "Quickly. Now!"

"Esmé, I can't take another woman or child's place," Matthew said, his eyes strayed to the boat.

"Listen to me. That boat is launching and there is room for at least another twenty people. Go with Olive. We'll find another. He won't take us all."

"Brother, go," Luke urged, before he pulled him into an embrace. "I love you."

"I love you too," Matthew whispered, choking back tears.

Once on board, Esmé, Luke, Violet, and

James, watched until Olive and Matthew were free from the ship.

"We need to find other boats and use the same excuse, I did for Matthew." Esmé faced Luke. "You and James are big, strong men. You'll have more strength than the young crewmen in the boats to row."

"I hope you're right. I need you to promise me that you'll leave regardless of me being on the boat with you," Luke begged.

Her eyes filled with tears. "I can't make that promise. I love you. I refuse to leave without you."

"I love you, too." Luke wrapped an arm around her shoulders. "Let's find a less crowded area to think."

They moved to where the first lifeboat had been launched, the area now abandoned.

"I think we should do what Esmé suggested," James said. "It worked for Matthew."

Could they be as lucky the next time? More passengers were panicking now.

. . .

1:40am

"Over there," Luke shouted, tugging Esmé in his wake as Violet and James followed.

"What is it?" Esmé had begun to panic because she knew they had less than an hour to get to safety. There was already a tilt toward the port side of the ship.

A lifeboat had started to launch with about ten passengers on board. Ridiculous!

"Please can we get in?" Luke begged.

The crewman ignored him, or didn't hear because of the noise.

"Please," Esmé pleaded. "Our husbands can row us quickly away from the ship, otherwise when the ship sinks, if we're close, we will be pulled with it."

The crewman lifted his head. Esmé gasped. "John?"

"I looked for you," he stated, as though he couldn't believe she stood before him. "All of you get in. Quickly!"

After a shocked pause, Esmé led the way into the lifeboat.

"John?" she questioned again.

He shook his head and climbed up messing with rope. Before she could say anything, the boat was being lowered. It felt like it took forever to finally feel the boat on the ocean, but it was mere minutes.

Luke and James helped John get the boat free of the ship before they quickly took an oar each and rowed them away from the rapidly sinking ship.

She felt numb. John was supposed to be with her but he'd disappeared in the crowd. And her thoughts had been on saving everyone she loved. But questions swirled around her and she needed answers to them. Only, she couldn't ask them in front of all the passengers. John knew. "I wasn't going into the water this time," he said, holding her gaze.

"I understand." She swiped at a tear. "Thank you."

John nodded. "Miss."

Violet huddled against her. "I wrapped up warm but it's so cold."

"We'll be warm and dry soon," Esmé reasoned. "Then we'll all meet up with Olive and Matthew, and exchange stories." She hoped that would be the case. She desperately hoped so.

The silence on the ocean, the further away from Titanic they got, became scary. The dark night surrounded them, with only the lights from the ship, lighting up the horizon. The cold seeped through Esmé's clothes and she couldn't stop shivering. As she breathed it left a trail of mist.

When they were a safe distance away from the Titanic, the lifeboat came to a halt. "We'll go back once the ship has sunk to help find survivors," Luke announced.

"I don't think that is a good idea. Certainly not safe for us," a woman in the back of the boat disagreed.

"If you survived the sinking wouldn't you want to be helped?" Esmé snapped.

Silence followed.

They watched in stunned disbelief as the huge ship slowly started to disappear.

Then the lights went out.

2:18am

. . .

To their astonishment, Titanic suddenly snapped in two. The sound was nothing compared to the shouts and screams coming from the ship, chilling her bones.

Esmé held a hand over her mouth as tears streamed down her face. Nothing had prepared her for what was happening as the stern sat on the water while the ocean had already swallowed the other half.

"Oh, my God," Violet gasped. "Those poor people."

"Should we go back now?" James asked.

Both Esmé and John shouted "No!"

Esmé realized she'd snapped. "We need to wait or we will be pulled in after it."

Luke slipped his hand around hers and held tightly.

2:20am

With a loud groan, the Titanic slowly started to rise into the night. Screams filled the air, as people slipped and fell to their death in the icy water.

The stern hung there, frozen in the cold air before it slid, rapidly—silently—into the ocean, disappearing from sight, leaving behind an eerie silence.

"We should go back now," Luke quietly suggested. "We need to be careful. We don't want to be rushed or they'll capsize the lifeboat." He squeezed Esmé's hand tightly.

There was nervous movement within the boat at the suggestion. It soon settled as Luke and James rowed back toward where the ship had disappeared beneath the icy water. Wreckage was everywhere, along with some dead—many of them appeared frozen.

Pain clutched at her heart over what she'd witnessed but she couldn't help feeling relief that her husband, and others had survived. She didn't think the thought was cruel, more like human nature.

It took a long time to search, but a few other boats could be seen in the distance. Their searchlights lit a path through the murky surface.

"I think that's it," John looked out but no sound could be heard. He turned to the others. "Let's head away from here. Not too far as we don't want the rescue boats to miss us."

After rescuing five passengers from the water, it took another thirty minutes to get the lifeboat clear of the debris.

Luke gently wrapped himself around Esmé, his face nuzzled against her neck.

No words were needed, as the despair all around them spoke for itself.

Esmé's eyes connected with John's, and she knew, without a doubt, he'd saved their lives. She mouthed, "Thank you."

He tilted his head to the side. "My future is unknown now."

Reaching out, Esmé grabbed his hand. "We all stay together John."

"I hope so, Miss."

Snuggled in Luke's arms, she felt safe. And she could believe that, now the disaster was over, maybe they would have the chance to grow old together.

She certainly hoped so.

CHAPTER 22
APRIL 15TH, 1912

3:10am

Esmé had never suffered seasickness before but her stomach was queasy after being in the lifeboat for several hours.

Luke's arms held her close even though his back must have been aching from sitting in the same position.

She glanced at Violet and smiled because her friend looked tiny with the way James protected her against the elements.

"We'll be rescued by morning," Luke said with confidence. "Or maybe sooner," his voice drifted off.

Esmé turned her head and followed Luke's gaze, which was off in the distance, on the horizon.

The Carpathia?

It wasn't the ship they could actually see, but lights, very slowly heading in their direction.

"Is that a ship Ma?" a young child asked.

"I hope so."

The child stared at Luke. "You were right," she said.

Luke grinned. "I always am."

Esmé laughed. "What's your name?" she asked the child.

"Lottie Sarah McCormick," she told Esmé with pride, slipping a smug grin toward her mother.

Her mother chuckled, a welcomed sound after the horrors of the night. "*Charlotte* Sarah McCormick. We're from Delgany, County Wicklow. My husband is waiting for us in New York." Her lip wobbled. "He's going to be so worried when he hears about the ship." She shook her head. "He worked and saved to get us second class passage."

"Don't cry, Ma. We will still get to Pa. You always tell me to have faith."

She smiled through her tears. "I'm Sarah, and as you already know this is my daughter. She's an eight-year-old handful."

The passengers in the boat shared their names, but Lottie, who obviously preferred that to Charlotte, was the most entertaining now that she had her second wind.

Question, after question.

Esmé took pity on the child's mother. "Lottie, tell me what you are going to do in New York?"

Lottie's red curls danced down her back as she became animated. "I am going to eat a large ice cream, and try lots of Italian food with my Pa. He promised to show Ma and me everything in New York. But I am going to have my own adventure to tell him now."

"That you will," Esmé agreed. "You have such beautiful hair."

"She gets that from her Pa's side of the family," Sarah added.

"It's getting closer," James announced, drawing Esmé's gaze back to the Carpathia.

Esmé's belly fluttered with nerves, and,

for once, she felt more confident that she would have a future with Luke.

7:22am

They dozed on and off but sleep wouldn't take them properly until they were out of the lifeboat, which would be imminent.

The Carpathia was maybe twenty feet away from them while they waited to be called closer to the boat.

Esmé would be excited if she weren't so tired and relieved.

It took another twenty minutes to get them on board. She nearly fell, her legs weakened through the cold and from sitting in the same position for hours.

"I have you." Luke wrapped an arm around her waist.

Two women on the Carpathia wrapped a blanket around each of them. "Please follow me," one woman requested.

"Violet and James?" Esmé asked, coming to a stop.

"Your friends are being looked after," she smiled. "I'm Josephine and I'm taking you both to my cabin." She paused. "You are married?" She frowned.

"Yes," Luke answered.

Josephine smiled and carried on down the passageway. Esmé exchanged a quick glance with Luke.

"Thank you for your help," Luke added. "I just want my wife to be warm."

"Can I take your names?" a crewman asked.

"Luke Carlisle and Esmé Carlisle," Luke informed him.

Esmé frowned. If her name was given, why hadn't she found it on the survivors' list when she'd researched back in New York? Surely, she would have seen her name next to Luke's.

"Thank you, Sir." The crewman ran off.

"This way," Josephine mumbled.

Overwhelmed with relief, Esmé felt close to breaking down as they followed the kind woman into her cabin.

"I've moved all my belongings into my sister's cabin. So please consider this yours until we arrive in New York…Tea and sandwiches will be here…" A knock interrupted her.

"Oh, here they are now." She placed the tray onto the table after taking it. "If you need anything, please let me know. I'm directly across from you."

"I don't know what to say," Esmé whispered, her voice breaking.

"No need for words." Josephine smiled and quickly left.

The room was small and the bed was slightly wider than a single bed but not by much.

"She was so kind."

"Yes." Luke sat her on the bed. "Let me pour us some tea, and we need to eat after everything that's happened."

"Okay. We need to look for Olive and Matthew as well," Esmé commented.

"They are still bringing passengers aboard, so we'll wait for now. I am no good to anyone exhausted." He glanced at the bed then the floor.

Esmé offered a small smile. "We are both sharing the bed. We'll snuggle."

"That's good because I need to hold you close." He yawned before he drank his tea down in a few gulps. "I didn't realize I was so thirsty."

"The tea is welcome." Esmé smiled, placing her cup down.

"I want you to hold me on the bed while we sleep." She kicked her boots off and removed her coat. Luke did the same and kept his pants and undershirt on.

Minutes later, they were huddled on the bed, arms wrapped tightly around each other, and legs intertwined.

"I feel as though I can finally breath again. Now I know we are safe."

"I love you, Esmé. I am thankful for a lot of things, but not as much as I am that you are safe here, in my arms, in my life."

She wiggled closer and buried her face in his neck. "I want to spend the rest of my life wrapped up in your arms Luke."

They clung together until sleep claimed them.

11:30am

. . .

Esmé hugged Violet so tightly; she ended up having to loosen her hold so her friend could breath. "I'm so happy we're together." Esmé pulled back. "We need to find Olive and Matthew." She bit worriedly at her lip.

"All names were taken so that might be the place to start," James offered.

"You're right," Luke said weary.

Esmé knew her husband was worried and she hoped they were alive and well on the Carpathia.

"I'll go and check."

"Not on your own, you're not." Esmé slipped her hands through his, clutching his arm.

Luke patted her hand, and said to the other couple, "We'll meet you back here in, say, thirty minutes."

"Okay, Luke," James agreed, a frown creasing his forehead.

Violet squeezed Esmé's hand as Luke led her away to locate his brother.

In the end, she wished they hadn't because they couldn't find Matthew and Olive on any lists.

She clasped Luke's hand tightly and asked the question Luke couldn't get out. "Are these complete?"

"Yes, Miss."

"So every single passenger who came aboard is on these? Correct? They were on a lifeboat."

The crewman dipped his gaze and said, "A couple of lifeboats capsized before we arrived in the area. We have been around the ship three times to make sure we haven't missed anyone. Everyone should be on the list unless they have purposely avoided us."

Esmé's eyes filled with tears.

"I'm so sorry for your loss." The man moved away.

"William?" Luke's voice broke, as he sobbed his nephew's name.

Esmé slowly led her husband into a more secluded corner. Her arms wound around his middle as she held him tightly against her. "I'm so sorry."

He said nothing, just tightened his hold

on her. Then she felt him shudder against her as the tears finally broke free.

She held him until he calmed and then watched as he wiped his face on a clean handkerchief.

"I'm…"

"No," Esmé quickly said, knowing what he was about to. "I know you, and you are not going to apologize for your grief." She reached up and cupped his face before kissing his lips. "I'm your wife and I love you very much. We are going to make sure William is always reminded of his parents. We will love him like our own." She smiled through her tears.

Luke inhaled, his eyes damp. "I think I'd rather go back to our room. I need to be alone."

Esmé tried to hide the hurt his words caused, but Luke caught it. "I'm sorry, I meant with you. I don't feel like being social." He glanced around them before holding her gaze. "I just want to be alone with you while I try and come to terms with what has happened."

She understood. "I'll meet you there. Let me go and tell Violet and James first."

"I should come with you."

"No. I will be fine on my own." She quickly kissed his lips. "I promise to be quick."

She watched Luke head inside toward the cabin they'd been given with his shoulders slumped in defeat. Tears hovered on her lashes as she watched him, her heart breaking.

She quickly blinked the tears away before she went to meet Violet and James.

CHAPTER 23

1987

"I'm nervous, Jake."

He stopped and cupped Sienna's face. After placing a kiss to her pink lips, he smiled. "I am too, but I'm also impatient to find out what happened to Esmé. It's like a story you read quickly to discover the outcome."

Sienna frowned. "I get that, but what if we don't like what Violet tells us? It's more than a story."

"You're right as always." Jake smiled.

"I like that you think I'm always right." Sienna flirted.

Jake laughed becoming serious as he caught Violet watching them through the window. He cleared his throat. "We've been spotted." He took Sienna's hand and led her inside.

"Just remember you're not alone," Jake whispered as he pushed the door to Violet's room open.

The elderly lady sat regal in her chair. The silver hair was in a neat bun at Violet's nape. Her hands lightly held a white, silk handkerchief.

"You look well rested," Sienna commented.

"I slept well and dreamt of my husband." She looked whimsical. "He is waiting for me, but he said I had to finish my story before joining him." A hand reached up dabbing at her eyes.

Sienna felt like crying her eyes out, and one glance at Jake's face told her he felt the same.

"So let me tell you." She sighed and waited for Jake and Sienna to join her.

"It was so cold on the deck of Titanic as we huddled together. Only Esmé seemed to know what we waited for. I certainly hadn't expected the iceberg or anything that followed.

"I'm not good at judging size or distance, but the iceberg was over a hundred feet tall and maybe three or four hundred feet wide. I've never seen anything like it before or since." She shivered and pulled her woolen wrap around her shoulders.

"When it became apparent that the ship was sinking, there was panic. Esmé made us all find lifeboats. She convinced them to let the men on board so they could man the oars. It wasn't that difficult when the lifeboat we arrived at was helmed by John, a crewman who happened to be a friend of Esmé. He told us all to board.

"In the end, it was James and Luke who rowed the boat to get us clear from the ship."

"Were Olive and Matthew with you?" Sienna asked, wanting to know what became of William's parents.

Violet shook her head. "Olive was pregnant so Esmé argued with a crewman and he allowed them on board one of the first lifeboats. It would have been too much begging for us all, so we found the one John had control of.

"In hindsight, I wish we'd waited and all boarded the same lifeboat because the one Olive and Matthew were on capsized. Neither could swim. We didn't discover this until we'd been on board the Carpathia for some time.

"Esmé blamed herself because she'd forced them into the boat. It wasn't and Luke told her that. They were stricken with grief. We all were.

"James looked after me, and then, days later, we arrived in New York, which was overwhelming." Violet wavered before she continued.

"In New York, a couple we had met during our wedding dinner, Scarlett and Edward became close friends of ours. Scarlett was a special friend. Between her and her sister, Martha, I learned how to design and sew ladies' evening gowns.

"Our store was popular for a very long time. We survived wars and the depression. Everything the economy threw at us. But, eventually, we became too old to keep up with demand and sold the store."

When the silence went on with Violet lost in thought, Jake asked, "What happened to Luke and Esmé?"

"Luke, I can tell you, but Esmé? I have no idea." She placed the handkerchief over her mouth and swallowed a few times.

"Luke became a recluse. He worked, but his heart was broken, and no one could mend it. You see, his wife, my beautiful friend Esmé, vanished on board the Carpathia as we sailed into New York."

"What?" Sienna gasped.

"No!" Jake hissed.

Jake was just as much invested in the story as Sienna was and he'd prayed Esmé had stayed with the man she loved. His own heart was slowly being repaired by Sienna, and he cared enough about Esmé to want her to have the love she deserved.

"How? What happened?" Sienna questioned.

"One minute she was there, and then she wasn't. The ship was searched but no sign of her. The outcome was that she'd fallen overboard and no one had noticed. Luke didn't believe that because she'd been with him and had only been out of his sight for five minutes. No one knew where she'd gone. He searched for a very long time."

"That's not true."

All eyes landed on the woman at the door. She looked younger than Violet, but not by much.

"It was all my fault and I never told anyone." Her body trembled as she joined them in the room.

CHAPTER 24
APRIL 18TH, 1912

8:00pm

The lights from the scout cruiser USS Chester escorted the Carpathia into the harbor at New York while Esmé was lost in thought. She fingered the letter in her pocket pondering the wisdom of her words to Luke.

"There's my wife." Luke's sudden interruption was welcomed as his arms wound around her middle. "What do you think of New York?" he asked, then added, "Pity we arrived in the evening."

Esmé held onto Luke's hands. "It's a

magnificent sight." She didn't admit to not noticing before.

"I'm not sure what it's going to be like at the house once I've told my parents, and William, about my brother," his voice caught, "and Olive."

"If you're worried about me then don't be. I will be there for you and them. Always Luke." She turned in his arms.

"What would I do without you?" He kissed her lips with a soft brush of his before resting his chin on the top of her head.

She pressed her face against the corded muscles of his chest and savored the moment. When she inhaled deeply, his scent filled her senses. This moment would be forever engrained in her memory no matter where the future took them or her.

"I'm scared Luke," she suddenly admitted, raising her face to his. "I have this bad feeling in the pit of my stomach."

"Oh honey." Luke cupped her face. "What are you scared of?"

She moaned. "Losing you." In one fluid motion, she wound her arms around his neck, and searched for his lips.

Luke groaned, his mouth covering hers hungrily, leaving her lips burning with fire.

A throat cleared.

Slowly breaking the kiss, Luke gazed into her eyes.

Overcome with love for her husband, Esmé buried her face in his neck, her heart raced as rapidly as Luke's.

"Thought it best to interrupt," James said, amusement in his gaze when Esmé chanced a glance at him.

She laughed, quickly kissing Luke on his lips. "I love you," she mouthed before glancing to Violet.

"Esmé?" Lottie shouted.

She smiled and waved at the eight-year-old child. "I'll be a moment," she whispered to Luke, a brush of lips against his ear.

Lottie had become a mischievous child on the ship, but everyone loved her. Around the corner from the deck, and out of view from the other passengers, Esmé found the young child in the stairwell.

"Ma says we're leaving soon. Will I see you again?"

"I will make sure to give you Luke's address before we leave the ship. I promise."

Lottie sulked "I'm going to miss you."

Esmé held her arms out to the child and smiled when Lottie jumped into them, clinging to her.

"I'll miss you very much Charlotte," Esmé admitted.

"Lottie!"

"I have to go," Lottie panicked at the sound of her mother's voice.

Lottie started to pull away and shouted, "Ouch!" reaching up to her head.

Esmé heard a low buzz. It reminded her of when she was in her apartment in New York just before she disappeared.

That couldn't be right?

The buzz grew louder.

Her head started to spin.

With fear in her eyes, she looked at Lottie, who had the look of frozen terror on her young face.

Esmé's vision started to blur.

She was leaving.

No! Not now!

Her hand reached into the pocket of her

coat and quickly removed the letter she hadn't realized she would need so soon. She tossed it at Lottie and pleaded, "Please give that to Luke." Her eyes begged before everything went black.

CHAPTER 25
1987

Jake helped the elderly lady into a chair close to Violet while they watched her quietly. She held Violet's gaze for mere moments.

"My name is Charlotte Sarah McCormick and I was eight-years-old when I met Esmé and Violet in a lifeboat after Titanic sank." Her eyes watered.

Sienna slipped her hand into Jake's. He glanced at her, and she gave him a small smile. "I'm okay." She gave Charlotte her attention. "Please go on."

"Esmé gave me attention. She would play games with me to let my mother rest."

She smiled. "My mother suffered badly with seasickness, especially after the ship sank.

"Esmé was my friend and in the end, it had taken me ten years to complete her final request.

"You see, as we were on our way into New York harbor, she came to talk to me after I called her over. I flung myself into her arms thinking I wouldn't see her again.

"As a child I had a head full of red curls and one had become tangled in the chain around Esmé's neck." Charlotte paused, distress in her voice.

"Would you like a glass of water?" Sienna asked, already pouring it.

Charlotte took the glass and placed it beside her on the table.

"Not only did the chain snap but the locket fell to the floor and snapped open.

"It was like magic. One minute everything was perfect, and then, the next, Esmé became blurred.

"I'll never forget the look on her face as she started fading in my vision. It was stark fear. She tossed a letter to me, begging for me to give it to Luke. Then she was gone, and I was left holding the chain. What I'd witnessed terrified me. When I snapped out of the unbelievable shock, I picked up the letter and locket.

"My mother found me in tears, holding both of them.

"She shouted at me, and only stopped when Luke appeared and took the locket and chain from me. He wanted to know where Esmé was and I told him I found it on the floor. I was scared I'd get into a lot of trouble because I didn't think anyone would believe what I'd seen.

"Esmé was never found as far as I know, and it wasn't until we moved house when I was eighteen that I found the letter Esmé had tossed to me, ten years before.

"Finding the letter was a shock." She took in a deep breath as though she was steadying herself. "I'm not proud of what I did. I opened the letter and read it. When I'd finished, my face was soaked with tears.

"I knew what I had to do, what I should have done on the deck of the Carpathia. It took me a week, but I found Luke and mailed the letter through his door. I didn't stay. I was too ashamed that I'd kept such a heartfelt letter from him for so long."

Stunned silence descended on the room, only broken by Violet's whispered, "What did the letter say?"

Slowly, with hands that trembled, Charlotte took a slightly browned piece of paper from her pocket. "I copied it before giving it to Luke."

Jake cleared his throat and accepted the letter. "I'm not sure how I feel about reading this, although I am curious."

"Once you read it, you won't ever be able to forget the words," Charlotte said before she turned to Violet. "We have been friends for years. I hope you will be able to forgive me for waiting ten years to give the letter to Luke."

Violet stared. "I understand, Charlotte. You were a scared child at the time. I won't hold that against you. Besides, you did right in the end."

Jake glanced at Sienna who nodded. "Go ahead."

April 17th, 1912

My Dearest Luke,

If you are reading this letter, then I have disappeared without a trace.

Please believe me when I say I would have moved Heaven and Earth to stay with you. To stay where my heart is. Unfortunately, accidents happen and that is the only explanation for why I have vanished as suddenly as I appeared. I would never have willingly done anything to take me from you.

No matter how strange this sounds, we first met in an Italian restaurant in New York, the year 1987. Yes, in the future my love. That is also how I knew what would happen to the Titanic, and all those people onboard. The wreck was discovered at twelve and a half thousand feet beneath the ocean in September 1985. The Carpathia

271

rescued Seven hundred and five passengers and crew, but more than fifteen hundred died.

After we had been rescued and were safe on board the Carpathia, I started to believe our future had been changed. By this time, we both know it hadn't, and that I had been dreaming.

I love you with every breath in my body and soul, and will count the moments until we are together again.

All my love,

Forever your wife,

Esmé.

Five minutes later, Jake said, "At the bottom of the letter, it says page one of three." He frowned and then turned to Sienna who was sitting next to him, her heart breaking before his very eyes. He wrapped an arm around her shoulders.

"So where did Esmé go?" Sienna questioned.

"That's a good question," Violet whispered, not really focused. "And why do we only have one page?"

"I didn't copy the other two pages. It was a list of things for Luke to do, to send her back to him," Charlotte admitted. "It was also further explanation about why she couldn't tell him before the disaster on the Titanic happened. She also told him about herself and her life in *her* New York.

"I wanted to copy all of her instructions but didn't want to risk it being found by someone else. It was risky enough with the letter."

Jake and Sienna didn't know what to say.

Violet had no trouble. "You both need to search for an Esmé Carlisle."

"By God!" Jake jumped up. "You're right. If she came back into a different time or even close to now, then there should be something to find."

He grabbed Sienna from the chair. "We need to leave." He turned to Violet and Charlotte. "We'll be back to let you know what we find."

"Don't be too long. I'm not as young as I used to be." Violet offered a slight smile, indicating for Charlotte to stay with a wicked gleam in her eye.

CHAPTER 26
DECEMBER 12TH, 1987

The fog in Esmé's head slowly started to clear but the voices made her heart pound. Without opening her eyes, she knew she was no longer with Luke on board the Carpathia. A flash of wild grief ripped through her and tears seeped under her closed lids. What would he think? Would he believe the words she'd written in her letter to him? Why was she so cold?

Very slowly, she opened her lids and stared at a white sterile wall.

Hospital?

It didn't stop the panic from rising in her as her eyes moved around the room. She franticly searched for a clue as to where she was. It slowly became apparent she *was* in a hospital. Inserted into the back of her hand was an intravenous cannula. She followed the small clear tubing to the drip, but had no idea what they were medicating her with.

Her clothing had been removed and she wore a thin hospital gown. She caught her breath and let the tears flow freely. All she wanted was Luke, and he was lost to her now. She'd never see his smile, hear his voice, feel his touch. For as long as she lived, she would never forget the way he'd looked at her, as though she was the only other person in the world.

A nurse quickly bustled into the room, looking like a gust of wind would blow her over with how petite she was. She glanced at Esmé and a look of sympathy crossed her face.

"Don't cry. It can't be all bad." The nurse grabbed a few tissues and passed them to Esmé. "I'm Colleen McCormick, and I'll be your nurse during the daylight hours." She had a pleasant smile. Just hearing the name McCormick made Esmé's heart race. Her age was difficult to guess but Esmé thought she was in her mid-fifties. Colleen had a head full of thick red hair that was neatly fastened into a braid down her back.

Could Colleen be related to Charlotte?

Too much of a coincidence?

While Colleen checked her pulse, Esmé asked, "What is the fluid?"

"It's a saline solution to help rehydrate you. Nothing to worry about." Colleen reassured her. A frown marred her brow as she checked all the lines and monitors. "There are two detectives outside your room who want to talk to you. One's my brother." She rolled her eyes. "He's retiring at the end of next week." She winced. "He's going to get underfoot and drive me insane."

Esmé cast a fearful gaze toward her door. "Why? What have I done?" Her voice broke on the words.

"Can you remember your name? It would be nice to not have to call you Jane Doe."

Confused, Esmé stared at Colleen. "Why would anyone call me Jane Doe?" She rubbed her forehead. "I'm so confused."

"You were rescued from the New York harbor. Damn lucky that worker on the docks saw you." She shook her head. "You were unconscious when they brought you in. No identification, no purse, nothing in your pocket. You barely had a pulse, so when they brought you in, you became Jane Doe."

New York harbor?

That was where she was when Charlotte had accidentally got caught in the chain. Is that why she ended up in the harbor?

After a pause, Esmé whispered, "Esmé Carlisle."

Colleen smiled widely. "What a lovely name. It's my middle name."

Esmé blinked, surprised. "Really?"

"It's unusual right? I was born Colleen Sarah Esmé McCormick." She smiled. "I took my maiden name back when I divorced."

Esmé's head was suddenly full of questions, but she didn't want the nurse thinking she was crazy. She even thought her story sounded crazy.

Colleen, unaware of the turmoil inside

of Esmé, fluffed her pillows. "I'll let the doctor know you're awake, and then I'll bring you a cup of warm tea and a slice of toast."

"Thank you." Esmé sighed. "I guess you better let the detectives in, although I don't know what they want from me."

"I think they want to know how you ended up in the harbor because no one saw you until that worker spotted you in the water. He told the detectives how, one minute there was nothing, and the next you were there." Colleen smiled. "I will admit to being curious, but I'm not going to pressure you. Why don't you wait until you've seen the doctor before talking to them?"

"I think I'd rather get it over with."

Colleen tipped her head and watched Esmé, before she agreed. "I'll tell them to come in. I'm only going to give them ten minutes."

"Wait!" Esmé suddenly had a thought. "What's the date?"

"Saturday, the 12th December." Colleen hesitated. "That's what you expected me to say, right?"

"What year?" Esmé's stomach rolled with tension while she waited.

Colleen frowned and took a step closer to Esmé. "1987."

Esmé couldn't control the sob as it burst from between her dry lips. She covered her mouth with a trembling hand. "I don't want to be here. I prayed this was a dream. I want my husband," her voice broke miserably as she cried.

Colleen tried to console her while Esmé cried until there were no tears left. "I don't know what happened, but I'll help you in any way I can. I think I'll stay while the detectives are here."

The nurse helped Esmé to and from the bathroom. Once she was back in bed, the door opened and the detectives entered. The tall one with a head of cropped, red hair edged with grey gave Colleen a pointed look, which probably meant for her to leave, but she held her ground and took hold of Esmé's hand.

"She's my patient, and not well enough to be badgered with questions."

"Now Colleen, you know me better

than that," the large detective commented. He grinned and turned his attention to Esmé. "I'm Detective Niall McCormick, and this is my partner, Detective Kelly Armstrong. We need to ask you some questions."

Esmé nodded. "My name is Esmé Carlisle, and I'm twenty-five, no six. I'm twenty-six."

"Can you remember how you ended up in the harbor?" Detective Armstrong asked. "There were no boats close by. No one had seen you on the docks."

"Could they have missed me?"

Detective McCormick shook his head. "Not in the clothes you were wearing. It looked like you'd been to a fancy dress party. Not from this time."

Esmé stared out of the window. "I can't remember any of it." She just wanted to sleep and wake up in Luke's arms. She swiped at a tear. "I just want to go home."

"What's your address? Is there anyone who will miss you?" Detective Armstrong asked.

"My husband is...is no longer here."

Esmé turned on her side and shut everyone out, her sorrow a huge, painful knot inside.

"I think it might be best to let her rest," Colleen suggested. "You have a name and age to work with, that should be enough for now."

Esmé had no idea what else was said because she closed her mind. All she wanted was her husband. To her, it felt like mere hours since she'd last seen Luke. Her memory of him was so clear while she hungered to be held against his strong body. Now, she had no idea how she would live the rest of her life without him.

Heaviness settled in her chest.

CHAPTER 27
DECEMBER 15TH, 1987

Esmé watched the large snowflakes fall to the ground from the warmth of Colleen and Niall's home. Colleen had driven her to the house in a large car meant for the snowy conditions before she'd turned around and headed back to work. Esmé hadn't moved in the hour she'd been there, comfortable in her surroundings. It had been a huge relief and weight off her shoulders when Colleen had offered her the guest room.

Why Esmé hadn't contacted Jake or Sienna, she didn't know, or maybe she did. Maybe they'd tell her it was all in her head, and she didn't want to hear that. She didn't believe that, not really. They were her only friends from this time so why wouldn't she contact them? It had been six months since she'd vanished. Would they know she'd found Luke? And what about Colleen and Niall?

Colleen and Niall puzzled her because she was convinced they were Charlotte's children. Somehow, she'd ended up with them. It wasn't such a common name. At least not that she remembered.

Her forehead pressed against the cold window while a permanent sorrow weighed her down—heavy on her chest. Even though she'd only spent days with Luke, she'd known from the moment they'd met that he would be forever engrained on her heart. She had never experienced a love like she'd shared with him, and the longing to be with him had caused a constant ache since she'd woken up in the hospital. She was positive her heart was broken.

Her musings were interrupted by a male voice. "Talk to me Esmé. I want to be your friend, and help you find what it is you're looking for." Niall smiled as he took a seat in one of the armchairs.

"I wouldn't know where to begin," she admitted. "Everything is jumbled and there are no explanations for what I've experienced." She offered a small smile, although she suspected it didn't reach her eyes. "Would you tell me more about you, and your parents?"

She'd surprised him.

"I wasn't expecting you to ask that, about my parents at least." He paused. "Maybe if I start with my mother?"

"Very inquisitive, Detective."

He laughed.

Esmé swallowed and asked, "Are you related to a Charlotte Sarah McCormick, who was born in either 1903 or 1904?"

Niall stared at Esmé and she got the feeling he already knew something. "How do you know of Charlotte?" He frowned.

"She's your mother?" Esmé sat forward on the cushion, anxious for his reply.

"Charlotte Sarah McCormick is my mother." He cleared his throat. "Esmé, how do you know my mother? From the residential home? Is that why she called and told me to get to the hospital?"

"I don't know how to explain," her voice quivered, "and I don't know how I ended up here, with her two children, when she was the last person to see me." Esmé stared at Niall but she didn't really see him. In her mind, she saw the child with a head full of bouncing, red curls.

Her lips tilted up in a smile. "I remember Lottie's red hair. She had so much."

"It thinned out with age." He smiled fondly. "It's all grey now."

Now.

Esmé sat forward and grabbed Niall's hand. "You mentioned a residential home. Is that where Lottie is?" She inhaled. "She knew I was in the hospital?"

He nodded. "Colleen wanted to take an early retirement and look after Mom here, but, in the end, Mom wanted to go to the residential home." He shrugged. "Mom can be forgetful, and a bit unsteady when walking, but she does okay. We both visit at different times during the week so she knows we haven't forgotten her."

He smiled and continued, "She's with a friend that she's known since childhood, so she's happy. That's really all we want for her...as to the phone call, over the years my mother has known things. She's never explained, and we just grew up knowing to listen. I guess I should admit to her calling Colleen, too, making sure my sister was your nurse."

She squeezed his hand and sat back in the window seat. "I don't know how to explain the phone calls or how your mother knew where I would be. It doesn't make sense."

Charlotte had been eight when Esmé had disappeared, so how did she know to send her son and daughter to look out for Esmé?

"What are you thinking?" Niall asked.

"I'm thinking," she paused, "that I'd like to visit your mother." She held his gaze. "It might be a shock...but I need to know how she knew to call you and Colleen."

"That has me more than curious as well. Why would it be a shock?" He sat forward, his elbows on his knees, his face deep with worry.

Her eyes pleaded with him to understand. "If I tell you now, you will think I'm crazy and should be in a psychiatric ward, not visiting your mother." Esmé winced. "But I promise, that if you take me to see Lottie, she will, hopefully, remember me, which will make my story less crazy." She grinned. "Or you'll just think your mother is as crazy as me."

Niall paused and then started laughing. "I have to see this." He tugged her up from the chair and out into the hallway. "Here," he said as he planted a brown woolen hat on the top of Esmé's head. "You'll need that." He checked her feet. "You already have boots on," he observed. He held a thick black jacket out for her to slip her arms into. "I'm sure Colleen won't mind you borrowing this."

A gust of cold wind and snow blew in the moment he opened the front door. He turned and took her hand. "Are you sure about this?"

"I think I should be asking if you're okay driving in this?"

"I'll get us there. It isn't far."

"Then I want to visit my friend." Esmé smiled. She was finally able to focus on something other than her despair—a way back to Luke.

CHAPTER 28
DECEMBER 15TH, 1987

The residential home was a large flat building that had been built in an L shape. Tall wrought iron lamps lined the pathway that led to the main entrance. Snow had covered the ground and the building. As Esmé turned to look out over the car park, she looked over the flat land. Farmland? It was freezing outside but the air was crisp and fresh.

"You are becoming a snowman," Niall said, dragging her indoors.

They stomped their feet on the rough mats just inside of the door. Niall hung their jackets up and then led her to the sign in desk. While he made small talk with the receptionist, Esmé glanced around the quiet area. It was comfortable with homey couches and chairs for visitors. A tall, green planter, decorated with gold Christmas lights, sat in the corner by the window, and a red and gold poinsettia sat on the coffee table with a selection of magazines.

"This way."

She followed Niall down a large hallway, which reminded her of a hospital—almost clinical. When Niall stopped outside a closed door, he turned to Esmé. "How big a shock?"

The nervousness in her belly felt like it was about to explode as she met Niall's gaze. "Hopefully not too big," she chewed her bottom lip, "but I'm not sure."

Niall nodded and, with a slight hesitation, started to open the door to his mother's room. "When were you friends with her?"

At Esmé's first glance of Charlotte, her *Lottie*, in over seventy years, she replied, "April, 1912," to Niall while her eyes stayed on Charlotte.

The elderly woman slowly turned from

the comfortable chair where she'd been looking out of the window—a thick blanket over her legs and a knitted shawl around her shoulders.

When Esmé got a full view of the woman's face, the image of Lottie as the mischievous child was all she saw. Overcome with emotion, Esmé gulped hard, hot tears slipping down her face.

"Is it you?" Charlotte whispered, her gaze clouded with tears.

Esmé nodded and took the seat that Niall pushed her into, opposite his mother. "You recognize, Esmé?"

His mother smiled, dabbing at her eyes with a handkerchief. "Yes," she answered and started laughing. "I haven't seen her in a very long time," her voice softened, "but she's exactly the same as she was when we met." She sighed. "I'm not though."

"Mom, can you explain the phone calls to Colleen and I, when Esmé was in the hospital? How did you know?"

Charlotte smiled softly. "I just knew she needed you both, and that you would bring her to me. I prayed Esmé would remember me and recognize your names. I especially told Colleen to make sure she gave Esmé her full name. I needed her to be led back to me without saying so directly."

Niall rubbed his brow. "You both have me confused and that usually takes a lot." Niall settled in. "Please explain how you know each other." He glanced as Esmé.

Esmé offered him a wry smile. "We met in a lifeboat on April 15th, 1912 as we watched the Titanic sink." She inhaled. "I can't explain why I was there, or how it was even possible. But I was there. Charlotte was eight years old."

Charlotte gave a slight nod. "And it was my fault that Luke spent years alone. I know that."

The distress Charlotte had was real so Esmé quickly jumped up and knelt at her feet. She took Charlotte's frail hands into hers. "It was an accident, Charlotte. I know that. If it hadn't happened when it had, it would have happened at some other point."

"I never thought I'd see you again."

"Will you tell me what happened after I vanished? Did you give Luke the letter? I mean, I assume you did because he did everything I asked."

Esmé dropped to her bottom and curled her legs under her. She followed Charlotte's gaze to Niall. Charlotte said to him, "I told you about Esmé, a long time ago. I don't think I mentioned her name, but I told you about the lady who vanished on the Carpathia."

His eyes widened and rapidly moved between his mother and Esmé. "Esmé?" He frowned. "You used to tell Colleen and me that story often when we were children." He shook his head. "Are you telling me that was a true story, and the woman is Esmé? That's what you're saying? You realize how that sounds, right?"

Charlotte chuckled. "Esmé Carlisle." She sighed, and said to Esmé, "I will tell you what happened, but then you have to do something for me."

"I will do anything for you to tell me about Luke," Esmé pleaded, her heart in her throat.

Settling back in her chair, Charlotte looked out of the window and stayed quiet.

Niall helped Esmé up and indicated the chair he'd been sitting on. "Sit." He smiled and then passed her a glass of water, placing another on the table for his mother.

"I was always full of energy. My mother told me that even in sleep I'd be moving around." Charlotte slowly started her story, her voice growing stronger as she became lost in the past. "We had nearly docked in New York, and I remember being afraid that I'd never see you again. You pulled me into your arms, and then I heard my mother calling. She used the tone of voice that told me I was in trouble." She smiled out through the window, and it was as though she thought she was alone.

"In a rush, I pulled away and felt a tug on my hair. Your chain was tangled in a curl. I'd broken it and heard the locket clatter to the deck. It popped open. I didn't really know what to do and froze." Charlotte rested her head against the chair, but turned her face to Esmé. "You became blurry and, seconds after you tossed me a letter, you vanished. I remember blinking a few times, wondering what I'd seen. You just weren't there. I quickly picked up the letter and shoved it into a pocket and then I bent for the locket just as Luke came around the corner with my mother.

"He took one look at the locket in my hand and he lost all color while his eyes looked around. He looked for you and became panicked. I honestly didn't know what to say. You vanished before my eyes, and who would have believed an eight-year-old child if I'd told that to anyone. I was terrified. It took five, maybe ten, minutes for the desperation in Luke's voice to get through to me.

"I told him I didn't know where you'd gone. I'd told everyone that one minute you were there, the next you were gone. That was the truth." Charlotte wiped at a tear as it slowly slipped down her wrinkled cheek. "I didn't give Luke the letter."

"What?" Esmé whispered, shocked. "Why?" She ignored the tears racing down her own face, and waited. "Luke knew what happened to me. He did everything I told him to do to send me back to him."

Charlotte nodded. "When I was eighteen, I found the letter and realized that I needed to make sure it was delivered. It was ten years late reaching your husband, but it reached him."

"Are you saying you were really in 1912?" Niall asked, sitting forward.

"She was there," Charlotte said to Niall. She turned her gaze on Esmé. "I know I should have given him the letter before we left the ship. Luke was frantic with looking for you. The ship was searched from top to bottom. I didn't know what happened after, but I've never forgotten the look on Luke's face when he realized you'd vanished.

"He loved you Esmé. I found a love like that when I was in my early twenties." She smiled softly. "Niall Fionn McCormick was a very distant cousin. He swept me off my feet. I didn't care that we had a loose family connection. I fell in love with him the day we met. I miss him." She glanced at Niall.

"I miss him too, Mom," Niall leaned forward and took his mother's hand. "He was a good father."

"Yes, he was." She smiled fondly. "He's been gone for a lot of years. No other ever interested me. It was him or no one. And I've been okay with that. You only have a love like that once." Her eyes strayed to Esmé. "You have to find a way back to Luke."

Esmé smiled through her tears. "I don't know how. I left the chain and locket behind."

Charlotte nodded slightly. "I'm going to have a nap, but I want you to visit the lady in the room next door before you leave."

Esmé frowned and turned to see if Niall had any clue as to why. He shrugged, standing. "There's only one room that she spends time in and it's to the left as we leave."

About to follow Niall from the room, Esmé glanced back at Charlotte. She quickly went to the child she remembered and kissed her forehead. "Thank you," she whispered.

CHAPTER 29
DECEMBER 15TH, 1987

"I don't understand why she would want me to visit with one of her friends." Esmé nervously reached out and knocked on the door.

When they heard a muttered, "Come in," Niall opened the door and ushered Esmé inside. He nearly knocked Esmé over with how she'd suddenly come to a stop in the doorway. Her gaze fixed on the elderly woman in the chair beside the window.

She only vaguely heard Niall talking.

It couldn't be. Could it?

"It's like seeing a ghost," the woman whispered, holding out a frail hand toward

Esmé. "Come closer so I don't think I'm going crazy."

Esmé's legs quivered as she made her way across the room. She felt frail and as though she'd aged those seventy-five years in only a few moments. She took her friend's hand and perched beside her. "I never thought I'd see you again." She quietly sobbed into a handful of tissues while Violet patted her hand.

"Holly, would you pass me the photograph, please?" Violet requested, and waved toward the woman in the room, "This is my great granddaughter Holly with her three children." Esmé watched her stare at Niall. "And you are Niall McCormick. Older than the last time I saw you."

Esmé chuckled and tried to hide it, but Niall caught her and grinned, a slight blush on his cheeks. He coughed. "Violet, it's nice to see you again. Just as pretty as always." He referred to how neatly presented she was.

The dress Violet wore was made from navy blue silk and looked out of this time. She had a dark and pale blue knitted wrap around her shoulders to keep the chill at bay.

"Grandma, we're going to go, but I'll be back tomorrow. *Alone,* okay?" Holly said, kissing Violet's cheek.

"I'm sorry for interrupting your visit," Esmé offered.

"It was time for us to go anyway, so please don't worry about it. These three need some dinner." Holly smiled and ushered her three young children from the room.

Violet sighed. "I love that girl, but she has her hands full." She turned her attention to Esmé and slowly handed her the photograph she'd asked Holly to pass to her.

"Oh," Esmé cried. "Luke," her voice broke as she stared at their wedding photograph. "I've only been away from him for a few days and I miss him so much."

Niall leaned over her shoulder and she heard him gasp as he took a closer look. "That's you," he whispered. "All this with my mother, and now Violet. It's all true."

"Yes," Violet acknowledged, her eyes never leaving Esmé.

"You disappeared on the Carpathia as it sailed into New York harbor," Niall thought aloud. "Is that why you ended up being fished out of the water? When you left 1912 there had been a ship where you were, but when you ended up back in 1987 there wasn't."

"I think so, but," Esmé said, a frown on her brows, "when I left here I was in my apartment in Manhattan, and I *landed* on the Titanic just as it was pulling out of Southampton. I don't understand the how or the why of all of this. All I know is that I was there. And I love Luke...that is real." Her eyes went back to the photograph in her hands. "How do I get back to you?" she asked Luke, caressing his face on the photograph.

Niall said, "I'm a bit at a loss as to how you managed to get from back then to now, or vice-versa. That makes no sense when I never thought it was possible to travel through time."

"It's a mystery that will never be solved," Violet whispered. "But I never thought I'd see you again," she said to Esmé, her voice full of wonder.

Heartbroken, Esmé said, "I don't know what I'm supposed to do with my life now. In a very short time, Luke became everything to me, and the thought of carrying on without him...I just can't."

"Would you go back to him if there was a way?" Niall asked.

Esmé could see the detective thought he'd lost his mind, along with them. She smiled reassuringly. If he was crazy, he was in good company. "I would go back to him in a heartbeat if I could. All I know is that the clothing and the locket were the trigger for me. I don't have either." Esmé stood and walked to the window, clutching the photograph to her chest.

The snow swirled around in the wind outside and Esmé had no idea what to do now. The life she'd wanted was lost to her, so was her husband.

Her breath caught at the back of her throat and she didn't even try to stop the tears that were sliding down her cheeks.

The loss was so great she didn't know how to move forward. She didn't want to be in her old life. She didn't belong here anymore. Body and soul craved what she'd left in the past, and without Luke in her life, she didn't even want to wake up the following day.

How could she ever explain how she felt? She couldn't because no one would ever understand. Probably wouldn't believe her either.

"Esmé," Niall said, reaching out to her. "You're freezing." He grabbed a blanket that Violet had pointed to, wrapping it around her shoulders. "Come and sit." He smiled. "I seem to be saying that a lot today."

She smiled through her tears and patted his arm. "You're a good man Niall Mc-Cormick."

"My wife used to think so." His sad words brought Esmé's attention up to his face. She searched and found a blank expression before he sighed heavily. "She died six years ago."

"You still miss her?"

"Every single day," he admitted.

Esmé squeezed his wrist and sat down

beside Violet. "I don't know what I'm doing anymore."

"You need to talk to John." Violet broke the silence. "He always knew more than he ever told anyone, including Luke after you vanished. I had a feeling he knew where you were, but when I asked him, he said he knew as much as we did. I never believed him."

"I saw him around over the years, and the last time, he looked as young as he did when we all met, so many years ago now." Violet frowned. "He can do the same as you?" She stared directly at Esmé.

It was true and there was no reason why she couldn't admit who John was. "John was born in the 1700s, and kept reappearing on the Titanic. He didn't know why, or how. All he told me was that I couldn't breathe a word to anyone about anything that I knew. If I did, I'd have been transported back to my time. The Titanic would still sink, and no one on board it would remember me.

"A huge part of me was selfish because I never wanted Luke to forget me, and the other part, knew I wouldn't be able to make a difference." Esmé offered a wry smile. "You see, John wasn't supposed to be on the lifeboat we used to leave the ship. He just refused to go down with the ship again. I don't think he was supposed to survive, but he did. I always knew he wasn't telling me everything, but I really don't think it was about the traveling through time. I think it was more to do with the future," her voice softened, trailing off as she really thought about it.

"What if John knows what happens now?" Esmé moved to the edge of her seat as words tumbled out of her mouth. "He might be able to take me back to Luke, or know of a way for me to go back without the locket." She took Violet's hands. "Do you know where he is?"

"No. I haven't seen him in years, but, I wonder..." Violet glanced out of the window before she held Esmé's gaze. "Jake and Sienna have been here wanting information about you. Something tells me your future lies with them and William."

Pained, Esmé admitted, "I was engaged to Jake, and I broke it off rather abruptly just before I disappeared. I don't love him and I'm not sure I ever did. He deserves someone who will love him the way I love Luke." She inhaled. "He is a good man, but he isn't Luke."

"Then don't worry about him because I think he's in love with Sienna." Violet smiled. "He was very concerned about her when we talked, and I may be old, but I'm certainly not blind." She smiled. "Go and see your friends. Ask them if you can go through Luke's belongings. Maybe there will be something there."

"I will." Esmé sat back and glanced at Niall when she had a sudden thought. "Why wasn't I on the survivor's list?"

"What do you mean?" Niall asked.

"When I was researching Luke and the Titanic, I checked the passenger list and there was no Esmé Carlisle or Esmé Rogers on the list. When I boarded the Carpathia I gave my name as Esmé Carlisle, or rather Luke did. I would have noticed if my name was next to his as they were alphabetical. So why wasn't my name there? That doesn't make sense."

Niall sighed, "Maybe because you disappeared before you docked in New York."

"No, they took your name down wrong." Violet shook her head. "On the survivors list, which I've seen, so had Luke, your name was taken as Esmé Lyle. Luke tried to get it changed but without you, they wouldn't change it. They flat out refused. He was so angry.

"I hope you find your way back to him, Esmé. You both deserve to be together." She smiled, sadly. "I will be with my James before the New Year. I'm looking forward to that. I've lived a good life, but I need to be with my husband now."

After a glance at Niall, who looked just as choked up as Esmé felt, she leaned forward and kissed Violet on the forehead. "Thank you and say hello to James for me." She paused. "If you see Luke, tell him I love him so very much." Her voice broke.

❧

"Let me just ask my mom something," Niall said when they left Violet's room.

"I'll wait in reception." Esmé smiled and walked away.

Niall inhaled deeply and pushed into his mother's room.

She turned sleepy eyes to his and smiled. "I knew you wouldn't let it go. You were always a curious child."

"I accept what you, Violet, and Esmé have said as the truth as you believe it to be. I don't know how, but what haven't you told Esmé?"

With a knowing look on her face, Charlotte turned to the window. "Everything has a meaning and we're trying to help Esmé without being too direct. The future cannot be spoken of." She turned and patted his hand. "Just be there and guide her where she must go."

CHAPTER 30
DECEMBER 16TH, 1987

The heat was on inside of Niall's car, but Esmé still felt chilled to the bone. She hadn't spoken much since they'd left the residential home the day before. There was nothing much for her to say anyway. Her throat felt raw and her eyes swollen with how emotional she was. Nothing felt or tasted the same without Luke. It was as if he'd died all over again.

Niall parked on the road outside of the house where it had all really started for Esmé—Luke's home.

A thick layer of snow covered the wrought iron railing in front of the large town house.

When Niall opened the car door for her, he helped her onto the sidewalk. "It's icy. Be careful."

She offered him a nervous smile. "Thank you for everything you're doing for me. I appreciate it."

He tsked. "You don't need to thank me." He knocked on the door. "Besides, I'm more than curious as to what happens next."

The door opened, and Jake was standing there in front of her. Color drained from his face as his eyes widened in shock. Esmé gave him a small smile as she took in his appearance. She was surprised to see him looking so rumpled; his hair needed brushing, his shirt hung out from the waist of his jeans. He cleared his throat and reached out to Esmé. "I thought I was seeing things." He pulled her into a brief embrace and indicated for Niall to enter.

Niall closed the door quickly to stop the snow from trampling everywhere.

"Sienna!" Jake shouted, and then looked unsure—almost nervous.

"I know about you and Sienna, and I'm

happy for you both." She patted his hand and accepted the warm hug from her friend.

"We've been looking everywhere for you." Sienna glanced at Jake. "Without much success I might add."

"I'll explain the best I can, but I need your help." Esmé grabbed Sienna's hand. "You will both help me?" she pleaded.

"If we can," Jake answered. "Of course we'll help you." He turned his attention to Niall.

Esmé vaguely heard them introduce themselves while Sienna led her into the living room. "Did you really go back to Luke?" Sienna asked before they'd had chance to sit.

Niall settled next to her, and Esmé slowly told her story. When she had finished, there wasn't a dry eye in the room. "I need to find John. Hopefully, he'll know how I can get back to Luke. I have to be with him."

"I don't know anyone named John." Sienna frowned, looking at Jake.

He shook his head. "It isn't a name we've come across while searching the past for more information about Luke and you, either."

"What about the attic?" Niall suggested. "Wouldn't papers that belonged to Luke be stored up there, especially as he owned this house back then?"

"We've been in the attic, searching for clues about you," Jake said to Esmé. "But we couldn't find a great deal."

The disappointment Jake felt at being unable to help her was apparent in the slouch of his shoulders. His frown deepened as his gaze landed on Sienna.

Tears hovered on Sienna's face and, while all eyes focused on her, a voice behind them said, "There could be papers at the other house."

Sienna blinked and quickly got to her feet. "Niall, this is William. He was adopted by Luke when he was two." She turned to Esmé. "You remember him?"

Esmé nodded.

"Hello everyone." He waved and drew his bushy brows together in deep concentration. "I don't think anyone has been there in years. A man," he paused, "Jonathan, looks after the place. Has done so for a very long time."

Esmé gasped. "Jonathan! Could that be John?" Her excitement grew.

"I don't remember anything about another house, and why wasn't it in with all the papers the lawyer had?" Sienna queried. "I was there with you and your son," she said to William.

"Hmm," he mumbled, and wouldn't meet her gaze when he added, "I don't remember," which told Esmé he knew more than he was saying. She glanced at Niall who raised a brow.

William continued, "There is a house in Stowe, Vermont that belongs to my father… I'll find you the address." He wandered off, deep in thought.

"I really hope he isn't letting his imagination run away with him," Sienna added, softly. "He's done that once or twice before."

"He appeared genuine," Niall observed. "Although, I think he knows more than he let on."

"Perhaps," Jake started, "the place in Stowe holds the key to what has been going on." He shrugged. "Someone, somewhere, must know."

William reappeared with a piece of paper clutched in his hand. "I have the address." He sat down and faced Esmé.

William shifted uncomfortably.

"Either way, I think we are about to visit the house in Vermont." Sienna took Esmé's hand and squeezed.

CHAPTER 31
DECEMBER 18TH, 1987

The large house was set back from the main road along a curved driveway. It was difficult to see many features of the landscape because of the heavy snowfall from the night before. Everything was blanketed in a heavy whiteness that was almost comforting. It was quiet and serene, and not really what Esmé had expected. Although, she hadn't given much thought to the kind of house Luke would purchase, she'd just set her heart on finding him.

Jake stopped the car out front while they sat looking over the place. Niall had stayed behind in New York with his sister, even though his curiosity was piqued.

No movement from the house could be seen, but Esmé did catch a horse and rider entering the stables to the right. She glanced at Jake and Sienna.

"Let's go," Jake suggested.

Esmé shivered from the chill in the air. And she felt so fatigued—her face pale and pinched, and realized that Jake and Sienna looked at her with concern. She couldn't fall apart because she needed answers first. Drawing in a deep breath, she admitted, "I'm terrified this will be a dead end and I will have to accept that I won't ever see Luke again." Her voice broke as she felt an acute sense of loss.

Sienna took her hand and held tight as they walked toward the barn. The snow crunched under their boots as they approached the tall double doors. A latch being set into place from inside followed by the slosh of water drew Esmé's gaze to the left. The back of a man faced them as the muffled thump of horse hooves were heard as he led the horse to the water trough. Seconds later the horse began to drink, and the man became aware he wasn't alone.

His heavy sigh could be heard at the door. "What can I do for you?" When he turned, Esmé caught her breath, worry eating her up.

It wasn't John.

When he approached, Esmé guessed he was in his fifties, over six foot tall with broad shoulders and a slim waist. He cleared his throat. "What's going on?"

"I'm sorry," Esmé stumbled over her words. "Is this the Carlisle place?"

"Who wants to know?" He crossed his arms and waited, but she didn't miss the recognition in his gaze before he quickly blinked, and it was gone.

Esmé glanced at Jake and Sienna, and she realized that they had decided that this was her show. She swallowed. "I'm Esmé Carlisle."

The man didn't look surprised. "I never thought…" he shook his head before running a hand through his hair. "I never thought that I would get to meet you."

Esmé frowned. "I don't understand. Are you Jonathan?"

"Yes." He smiled. "My father always spoke fondly of you."

"John," she whispered.

"He was a good man. Different from most." Jonathan smiled and indicated for them to follow him toward the house. "Who are you two?" he asked looking at Jake and Sienna.

They introduced themselves as he led them into the cozy kitchen. "I don't live in this house because it belongs to you," he said to Esmé, "but, I do look after it, and keep a few supplies here for when I'm working long days."

"Belongs to me?" She rubbed her brow, a headache forming.

"How long has the house belonged to Esmé?" Sienna enquired, only giving Esmé a quick glance.

"About sixty or so years, I think. It was before I was born anyway." He poured them coffee without even asking what they drank. "My father talked about you," he said to Esmé. "He always said that he wouldn't have had the life he'd managed to live if it hadn't been for you helping him change his future." He took a gulp of the hot coffee, too hot for Esmé. "It took me a long time to understand what he'd meant."

"Did you ever meet Luke?" Jake asked.

Jonathan paused and let the silence settle, before he admitted, "Yeah, I did." That was all he offered.

"Was he alone?" Jake persisted.

Jonathan glanced at Esmé, and hesitated before he replied, "Yes."

He lied. Why?

The silence was painful. Knowing Luke had been to the house with another woman hurt. It hurt more than she could bear. In a rush, she quickly stood. "I shouldn't be here. I need to leave."

A hand reached out and grabbed her wrist. "Wait," Jonathan snapped. "I never said who he was with, so don't go jumping to conclusions."

With a hand that trembled, Esmé wiped at the tears flowing from her eyes. "I just want to be with him. For me, it has been six days since I last saw him, and when he died," she paused to control the sob that nearly burst free, "he'd been without me for over seventy years. I want to go back to him and be by his side. I just don't know how."

Jonathan held her gaze and kept hold of her wrist. "I need to talk to you alone." He turned to Jake and Sienna. "There are sandwiches and cake in the fridge. Help yourself to them and more coffee." He finally let go of Esmé and indicated for her to follow him from the house. "It's cold out here, but I need to take you somewhere." He glanced at her feet. "At least you have on suitable footwear."

Large snowflakes were falling as he led her around the back of the house and toward the line of trees further back from the property. She hesitated and glanced at him, uneasiness slowly creeping up her spine.

He offered a wry smile. "Don't be afraid. I'm not going to hurt you. Just send you back to Luke."

She stumbled and stared. "What?" she whispered. "How?"

He turned around to face her. "I'm not one for talking or being around others. I like it that way. All I know is what my father told me to do if you ever showed up here.

He always knew more than Luke, which would cause big arguments between them. My father knew everything." Jonathan grinned.

He left her in his wake. She ran the best she could in the thick snow so that she wouldn't lose sight of him. They entered through the trees and walked for more than twenty minutes before Jonathan took her arm, and stopped.

"I can't go any further." He turned her to face him. "When you walk through the two trees behind me, keep going. You'll know when you are back." He glanced away. "Please don't ask me how or why because I don't know. I think my father did, but he never told me."

He glanced back at the trees and then turned to Esmé. "I was told to tell you that, by the time you get back, you will have been missing for four years. It will be 1916. But Esmé, when you go back, you will stay in the past. There are no more triggers. Nothing. This is your only chance to be with Luke for the rest of your life. Do you understand me?"

"Yes." Was it the truth? Could it really be so easy for her to be with her husband again? "Will I be able to tell him the truth about what happened to me?"

He nodded, a small smile slipping to his lips. "Yes. You'll be there permanently."

She took a moment to reflect on his words and then, before she could think, Esmé hugged Jonathan, much to his surprise, and ran toward the two trees he'd indicated.

The snow frustrated her but her desperation to get back to Luke won through any obstacle. Then she was standing between the two trees. The sound of a swarm of bees buzzing around her head grew stronger and she stopped and turned to face Jonathan. She watched as he dropped to his bottom before the image of him became blurred. Esmé too dropped to the cold snow, as the dizziness grew stronger, bolder. Everything momentarily went black and then she felt as if she was falling seconds before everything around her became silent—still.

CHAPTER 32
JULY 12TH, 1916

The ground beneath Esmé no longer felt cold and wet. Instead, it was hard and warm. She looked up and let the rays from the sun warm her face before she slowly peeled her lids open and glanced around. But for the snow having cleared, she would think she hadn't gone anywhere. However, she was now in a different season. The sun burst through the branches of the trees, heating her completely in her winter jacket and thick boots.

A tree root dug into her bottom as she slowly used the trunk of a tree to guide her to her feet. Her legs felt unsteady and her head swam before her eyes stopped blurring. Did she dare to believe she'd done it? Had she really arrived back to find Luke?

Before her brain followed, she started walking back the way she'd just come with Jonathan. He was nowhere in sight. Her legs gained strength as she picked up speed, almost stumbling on the roots from the trees. Of course, they had been buried under thick snow the first time she'd taken the path.

At the first sight of the house, Esmé stumbled to a stop, grabbing a branch to prevent herself from ending up on the ground. The house looked the same, although she could see it was painted a pale yellow with white trim. It looked and felt quiet, as though there wasn't anyone around. She prayed she was wrong.

Slowly moving forward, Esmé glanced to her left, and felt the skin at the back of her neck prickle as though she was being watched. She shook it off and went around to the front of the house.

Why was it so quiet?

Her heart raced as she glanced at the front door before she slowly pulled it open and entered. Someone had to be home.

A sudden noise from the kitchen caught her mid-step, so she took a chance and called out, "Luke?"

The noise ceased.

"Luke?" she shouted louder, seconds before she heard a crash followed by a curse.

She dashed to the kitchen and caught an angry, "I'm imagining her again," muttered under his breath. She watched as he fell to his knees, his shoulders stooped as he started shaking. He fell over to his bottom, which is what made Esmé move.

Luke must have sensed movement because he looked up and smiled through his tears. "I'm even seeing you when I'm awake now."

"No," Esmé said, dropping down and taking his hands in hers. Tears ran, unchecked, down her face while she watched Luke stare at her. "I'm real, Luke." She climbed on his lap, wrapping his arms around her waist as hers went around his neck. She tightened around him in an embrace she never wanted to end. "I never wanted to leave. It was an accident, which I'll tell you about later." She kissed his ear, his neck and finally cupped his face in her trembling hands. "I am real, Luke. Touch me. Feel me. I love you."

"Esmé," he breathed her name against her lips, while cupping her face. He swallowed hard.

"I promise," she kissed his palm, "that I am as real as you are."

His fingers gradually caressed over her eyes, her cheekbones, and hovered over her lips. "Why did you leave me? Where did you go?"

She gasped for breath through her tears. "It was beyond my control." She smiled. "I will tell you everything but, first, I need you to hold me. Promise me that no matter how crazy my story sounds, you will believe me."

Suddenly embraced in Luke's strong arms, Esmé gave in to her relief and sank into her husband. He meant more to her than anyone and she was scared she'd wake up and it all to have been a dream.

"Do you think you can stand?" Esmé asked, moving from Luke. She held her hand out to him.

"What are you wearing?" he asked, staring at her jacket.

She removed it. "I'll explain later."

He paused and nodded. "I never gave up hope, that you would find your way back to me," he admitted, intertwining their fingers together. "Let me show you our room." He offered a sheepish smile.

Upstairs, the main bedroom at the front of the house was spacious and comfortable. Luke watched her take her time moving around the room, taking it all in. A sideboard sat to one side and held pictures of them from the Titanic in beautiful frames.

A white bedspread with small rosebuds covered the bed. On the small table, on Luke's side of the bed, was a smaller wedding photograph.

"I haven't really been living without you." The wedding band on Luke's finger caught her attention as he ran his hands through his hair.

At that moment in time, nothing else mattered apart from them. Esmé flung her sweater across the room and reached for Luke.

She breathed, "Make love to me," against his lips seconds before his mouth covered hers hungrily. His kiss was urgent and searching. When he carried her to the bed, she felt as though she floated on air.

Luke trembled as he raised his mouth from hers, and gazed intensely into her eyes. "I love you, Esmé. Only you. Always. I have never stopped."

He reclaimed her lips, crushing her beneath him. She didn't care. She'd missed him and never wanted to be separated from him again.

A trail of fire followed his lips as they moved down her neck to her chest. "I don't know what this is, but I like it," he growled in reference to the stretchy tank top she wore.

Large hands gently outlined the circle of her breasts, which caused them to surge at the intimacy. His head dipped as he nibbled the sensitive nipples poking through her top.

Esmé wrapped her legs around his hips, wanting to feel the hardness of Luke.

He suddenly yanked her top off, letting

it sail through the air as he moaned at the sight of her bare, quivering breasts. With an unsteady hand, he unfastened her jeans and pulled them, along with her panties, down her legs. He quickly removed his own clothing and lowered his body over hers.

Their mutual gasp of arousal was lost as the blood rushed through Esmé's ears. Luke was everywhere. Consuming all of her. She couldn't get enough of him as her hands caressed over his back to the firm cheeks of his bottom. He shuddered at her touch. Cursing when she slipped a hand between them, and wrapped her fingers around the rigid flesh between his legs.

"Love me," Esmé pleaded, tugging him closer so they could join.

He plunged inside of her and hissed, "Always."

He held still, his breath as heavy as Esmé's. Their eyes locked as he slowly started to make love to her.

Tears rolled down her cheeks as Luke placed a tender kiss to each of her breasts.

She threaded her fingers into the back of

his hair and brought his mouth to meet hers. His eyes glazed as his mouth parted and he kissed her as though he was devouring her.

He aroused her beyond the point of return as she surrendered completely to the passion Luke created with the slide of his flesh, and the feel of their slick bodies rubbing together.

Her body began to vibrate with liquid fire and, as she held Luke's gaze, a tremor inside heated her thighs and groin, and hurtled her over into a climax beyond anything she'd ever experienced. Eyes closed, she gasped. Straining against Luke, she felt him reach completion too.

Time seemed to move in slow motion until Luke gathered her into his arms and settled her against his chest, their legs entwined.

"You are wearing my locket," Esmé said, fingering the item that had taken her to Luke in the first place. She'd felt it against her chest as Luke had made love to her.

"I've never taken it off since I had it repaired. I have no plans to either."

"I'm so sorry, Luke." She kissed his shoulder.

Very quietly, with his fingers stroking circles on her back, Luke asked, "Did John know you were coming back to me today?"

The hand that rested on his chest stilled, and Esmé lifted her eyes to his. "I haven't spoken to him, but he knows everything." She closed her eyes and kissed his chest. "Tell me why you would ask that, and then I'm going to tell you every little thing about me, and explain how I vanished from the Carpathia."

Esmé rested her chin on his chest and felt delight at the gentle brush of his fingers on her shoulder. "John lives here, and he told me I *had* to be here today. He was adamant."

"How did John end up here?"

He raised a brow at her asking another question, when she'd promised just one. He still answered, "When we couldn't find you on the ship, something told me to keep John close. He had nowhere else to go, so he came with me. At first, I thought he was in love with you, but then he admitted the only feelings he had for you were sisterly." He smiled. "Eventually, John was the only one I could talk about you with."

Luke closed his eyes and inhaled. "I've missed you. Every second of everyday, Esmé."

"This time I'm not going anywhere unless it's with you." She moved closer and buried her face in his neck. "Let me tell you what happened to me..."

EPILOGUE

JULY 2017

Jake stood with his arm around his wife of twenty-nine years as they watched the removal truck depart. It had taken both Sienna and him by surprise when the letter from the Boston lawyers had arrived. Bequeathed to them by a Jonathan John Sutter. The Jonathan they'd met thirty-years ago— never to have talked to since.

Sienna had been insistent that Esmé had had something to do with the bequest. Maybe she had.

The years had passed since they had both last seen Esmé, and it was at the very house they were the new owners of in Stowe.

Jake had wondered about Esmé over the years, but he had agreed along with Sienna to not look into the past anymore. It had been difficult to let go at first but their lives had moved forward. And it had become easier.

Their two sons, Richard and Stephen, even at the age of twenty-four, and twenty-seven, had no idea about Luke and Esmé.

He wasn't even sure where he would begin to tell the story about the couple. Some things were meant to stay in the past —*like Esmé.*

He gave a heavy sigh and smiled when Sienna reached up and kissed his cheek. "Let's go and eat before we do anything else," she suggested.

They walked into the house and found their sons at the kitchen table. Lots of old photographs spread over the top of it.

"Look what Rich found shoved at the back of the closet in the master bedroom," Stephen said, excited. "They were in an old shoe box."

Jake sat down heavily on a chair as shock

raced through him. He recognized the woman on many of the images.

"Oh," Sienna joined them at the table, selecting a picture. "It's can't be..." her voice trailed off.

"You can't know them, Mom. On the back of the one you're holding it's dated 1922," Richard commented and frowned. "Mom?" He glanced at his father. "Dad?"

Jake riffled through the images and started laughing through the tears running from his eyes and down his face. He took Sienna's hand. "She found a way to let us know she had a life with Luke."

Sienna nodded as they both continued to look at all the photographs. They told a story they couldn't even have imagined.

"This looks like it was taken in Ireland," Stephen said, turning the image over. "Cobh, 1928."

"And this," Richard said. "Disneyland, July 1955."

Jake gently took the photograph from his son and wiped his eyes. "I think that must be William and his wife, and is that David?" Jake pointed them out to Sienna.

"It must be," she whispered.

Moments later, Sienna gasped. "Look, she lived to be an old lady." Sienna held up a photograph of Esmé and Luke, dated 1985. Sienna cried. "When I first started working for Luke, I was told he'd just lost his wife of many years. No one at the hospital knew exactly how long they had been married. I had no clue it had been Esmé. She died in August and I started as Luke's caregiver in October of the same year."

"You two are not making much sense," Stephen grumbled.

Richard chuckled. "They never do."

Jake glanced at Sienna before they both turned to their sons, who watched them carefully. "I think," Jake smiled, "it's about time your mother and I told you about Esmé and Luke Carlisle because I don't think they want to stay in the past any longer."

THE END

337

DEAR READER

Thank you for reading *Come Back to Me,* and thank you for your reviews! It's really appreciated.

Subscribe with your email to be alerted about new releases, sales, and events. http://ronajameson.com/suscribe

SNEAK PEAK

SUMMER AT ROSE COTTAGE

SUMMER AT ROSE COTTAGE

CHAPTERS ONE TO THREE

CHAPTER ONE

"Auntie Mack, are we there yet?"

Mack smiled, and glancing through the rear view mirror saw how bored her nephew, Lucas, was. He hadn't even lasted thirty minutes before the 'are we there yet' questions had started. "Not yet, but it won't take us long. I promise."

With a dramatic sigh, he turned and stared out of the car window.

Mack hid her amusement while her heart filled with love for him. He'd been in her heart from the moment her sister had given birth to him, and now he was a mischievous six year old. His parents, Melinda and Daniel, were scheduled to fly to Europe later in the day, which was why Lucas was spending time with her in Cape Elizabeth.

For the first time in her working life, Mack had splurged on a summer rental—Rose Cottage. Being a teacher worked out well because it made it easier for her to take the summer out of the city.

It would certainly be a change from her matchmaking parents who wanted to see her married with a child of her own. She was only in her twenties and had no idea what the rush was all about.

Another heavy sigh from the backseat brought her thoughts back to Lucas. She knew what was coming…

Three… Two… One…

"Are you sure we're not there yet?" Lucas asked again, fidgeting in the backseat.

Her lips twitched with amusement, as she replied, "Lucas, we'll be there soon. Why don't you read one of your books?"

"Auntie Mack, my books are boring. Can I read one of yours?" He bounced up and down in his seat full of excitement at the thought.

"My books are for adults and they have no pictures in them." Thank goodness her books were packed in the trunk so Lucas couldn't go rooting around for them.

"But Daddy told Mommy that she would learn a lot if she read the type of books you read, instead of her boring magazines. I like to learn," Lucas replied with his 'cute' face.

Her eyes filled with amusement because Lucas knew that his Auntie Mack had never been able to withhold anything from him when he gave her that look. He obviously hoped she would give in and let him have a rummage around in the box of her things. The more she thought on it, she started to blush, wondering what type of books Daniel thought she read. "They're still adult-only books, Lucas. If you're bored with yours, why don't I buy you some new ones when we get there?"

"As soon as we get there? You promise?" Lucas tossed his current books onto the spare seat beside him.

"We'll check the stores out in a day or

two." With a quick glance through the mirror, she saw that Lucas's face had started to fall, so she added, "But if you're good until then, I'll buy you that atlas you wanted, then you can keep track of where your parents are staying in Europe."

Lucas thought about what she'd said and smiled in agreement. "That would be cool."

"Now that's the end of that. Why don't you have a nap? I'll wake you when we get there. That way, the time will pass super quick."

Five minutes later, Lucas was fast asleep, and then over an hour later, Mack pulled up outside of Rose Cottage, cutting the engine. The quiet and stillness must have woken Lucas because he shot up in his seat, hitting the side of his head against the window with a dull thump. "You all right, Lucas?"

He rubbed his head. "I think so. Are we there yet?"

"Yes, we are, thank goodness... Let's stretch our legs." She peered across the yard and spotted a man walking toward them at a leisurely pace. He was of medium height, slight build with short dark grey hair. As he moved closer, she could see that his bronzed face was weathered from the wind and sun. "In fact, I think I can see Mr. Degan on his way to the cottage." Mack pointed to the left, assuming he was the landlord for the summer.

She climbed out of the car and opened the back door for Lucas. He jumped out and ran around her in excitement before he ran to greet the owner of Rose Cottage.

As she watched him dash toward Mr. Degan, she suddenly thought better of it as there was no telling what would come out of Lucas's mouth, so she jogged over to them. "Mr. Degan?" Mack questioned, holding her hand out. "I'm Mackenzie Harper, and this is my nephew, Lucas Cartwright."

"You like fishing?" Mr. Degan asked as he released her hand.

"Um, not really," she replied. Her brows came together in confusion at the odd question. No welcome, just fishing. There was no way she was going anywhere near the bait…and pulling the fish from the water wasn't appealing either.

"I wasn't talking to you, young woman. I was talking to this here imp." Mr. Degan pointed at Lucas.

Lucas was jumping up and down like an excited puppy. "I've never been fishing, but Daddy says you have to try everything once."

"Mmm, there are some big suckers in the river. I thought I could use you as bait?"

Lucas looked confused while Mack's eyes nearly popped out of her head. "Mr. Degan, I don't . . ."

"Calm yourself. I'm only pulling your leg. Please, call me Thomas. I may be in my eighties, but hearing you say Mr. Degan makes me feel like my father."

Mack smiled and decided it was probably a good idea to change the subject. "Do you have the keys?"

"No need," Thomas replied. "The door's open." He walked to the cottage with Lucas, who seemed instantly at ease with the older man, slipping his hand into Mr. Degan's. For her part, Mack didn't really know how to take Mr. Thomas Degan.

Mack caught up to them in the kitchen.

It wasn't at all like she'd imagined when she'd read the description online. But it was a pleasant surprise. It was large and airy with white cabinets that looked to be older than she was but were still in good shape. The countertops looked to be a fairly new beech wood. The flooring was patterned linoleum in yellow and white. A hanging rack filled with pots and pans, a flowery ceramic jar with cooking implements poking out of it sat to the side of a large wooden chopping block. She certainly didn't miss the coffeemaker next to a wooden stand with hooks, holding coffee cups.

As Mack approached the stove for a closer inspection, she decided a bit of caution would be used before she so much as switched it on. The stovetop had been scrubbed clean, and reminded her of the one in the house where she'd grown up.

Turning back to Thomas, she asked, "Have you always lived around here?"

He scratched his chin, appearing to be deep in thought. "My parents settled in this country around 1924 after sailing over from Ireland. They went to New York first but moved here into Rose Cottage in 1927. Of course, back then, and as a child growing up, it was known as 'Degan House'."

"Perhaps you could spare some time and tell me more about your parents? Perhaps come over for coffee and homemade cake?" Mack hoped the food offering would tempt Thomas.

He took his cap off. "Hmm."

Thomas seemed nice, especially since he didn't seem to mind Lucas hovering. In fact, Lucas had made a new friend by the look of things.

"Thomas, I have pizza in the cooler and there's plenty of it, too much for the two of us really, if you'd like to join us for dinner?"

The minute Thomas perched on the old kitchen stool, Lucas climbed up onto his lap. "Please stay, Mr. Degan."

"Don't mind if I do," Thomas answered, grinning at Mack. "I'll keep this little jumping bean occupied while you unload, if you'd like."

"That would be great, thanks. We don't have too much with us, so it shouldn't take that long."

Standing outside, she looked around and took in the clear view of the ocean and the cliffs with the cylindrical domed lighthouse perched on the edge of the headland, the rotating light at the top flashing as it comes around.

The cottage was surrounded with bursts of vibrant colors; red and yellow roses, marigolds, cone flowers, and sunflowers. Flowering trees and bushes offering snowball-sized bursts of blue and white hydrangea, heavy purple cones of fragrant lilac. Trellises covered in flowers displaying the summer.

A wrap around porch had planters and hanging baskets providing even more bursts of color. Adirondack chairs where at the back, facing toward the ocean.

A gazebo sat at the end of the back garden, which would be a good place to sit and be sheltered from the sun to keep an eye on Lucas while he played and she read or relaxed with a cup of coffee.

Taking a deep breath of the fresh, salt air, she felt relief that she hadn't inhaled a lungful of car fumes in the process, like she did most days in the city. Not only did everything smell fresh, it was also blissfully quiet. No car horns and no noisy neighbors. It was just the sound of the waves on the shore, the wind in the trees, and the birds singing around them. It was simply paradise to Mack.

So with a spring in her step, Mack began emptying the car, taking short trips back and forth, as she carted Lucas's toys, their clothes, and books into the quaint cottage.

The last trip inside was with the food, and it was only after she'd put it away in the cupboards and refrigerator that it dawned on her how quiet the cottage was. Lucas was six—he didn't do quiet.

Mack listened and heard voices upstairs.

With the lid snapped on the cooler, ready to be thrown back into the car, she collected a box of clothes from the bottom of the stairs and headed up. After quickly placing the box in what she presumed to be the master bedroom, Mack opened one of the doors and found them both sitting down on one of the twin beds in the bedroom. Thomas was reading what looked to be a very old comic to a grinning Lucas.

Thomas caught sight of Mack and waved the comic up in the air. "Lucas found it underneath the closet, along with some spiders." He chuckled.

Mack looked nervously around her. "Spiders?" she questioned a laughing Thomas.

"I think I'll leave you two alone for now. I'll give you a shout when dinner's ready." She was still looking for spiders as she shut the door, hearing Thomas and Lucas laughing as she retreated downstairs.

She was such a wimp!

"Thomas! Lucas! Dinner is ready. Please wash up," Mack shouted from the kitchen.

After fiddling about with the aging but clean oven, she finally produced a nicely warmed pizza.

Slicing it into small, evenly sized triangles, she arranged them on a serving plate. As Thomas and Lucas appeared, she placed the pizza alongside the potato salad on the table

"Take a seat. What would you like to drink, Thomas?"

"Water's fine," he replied while helping himself to pizza and potato salad.

After she'd poured everyone a glass of water, Mack finally sat down, joining the two obviously hungry boys.

"So, you folks always lived in Boston?" Thomas asked around a mouth full of pizza.

"Yes. Born and bred there, Roslindale specifically."

Lucas turned and grinned at his Auntie Mack before he turned back to Thomas. "She's a schoolteacher and frightens all the kids in the class," he blurted out.

"Lucas, don't talk with your mouth full, please."

"You and Mr. Degan just did," Lucas replied indignantly with a cheeky smirk.

"Well, Mr. Degan and I are very naughty then, so you behave." She chuckled.

"Is she always this bossy?" Thomas grinned at Mack.

Lucas shoveled in more food and said

around a mouthful, "You really have no idea. You should be thankful she isn't your auntie."

"Hey, I can always take you back to Boston. You can stay with your grandparents," Mack replied sternly, while trying not to laugh.

"No way. They are old and no fun. All they want to do all day is play cards." When he noticed the frown on his Auntie Mack's face, he added, "And strip poker."

Mack choked on her drink. "They do no such thing, young man. Well, maybe cards." She glanced across to Thomas, who was trying to eat without laughing.

Lucas was so funny with the things that came out of his mouth on occasion. She could see why Daniel always watched what he said around Lucas. Melinda probably wasn't as careful, and Lucas's grandmother, obviously, wasn't careful at all.

The rest of the meal was eaten in comfortable silence, and before she knew it, Thomas had cleared the table and started to fill the sink with water and dishwashing liquid.

"Thomas, you don't need to do that." Mack stood to help.

"I know I don't need to do this, but I want to. Why don't you get some coffee going?" he said with a twinkle in his eye.

Laughing, she turned to do his bidding. While Mack waited for the coffee to brew, she followed Lucas into the living room and switched the newly setup Wii on for him. He was allowed thirty minutes each evening before bed.

With the dishes all washed and dried, Mack joined Thomas at the kitchen table, hoping he wouldn't mind telling her about his past. She really enjoyed hearing about people's lives, especially before and just after the Second World War, and with Thomas, she already felt comfortable enough to ask him questions.

"Would you mind telling me something about your parents? What were they like? What did they do?" She grinned at Thomas, who looked as though he'd never been asked that before. "Sorry, I find family history rather interesting." She blushed.

He frowned and gazed into his mug of

coffee. "My parents, hmm. Well, my mother and father, Josephine and Thomas, were both born in Delgany in County Wicklow in 1899 and sailed for America in the early 1920's on the RMS *Mauretania* from Southampton to New York."

"I've always wanted to visit Ireland, but it would mean a rather long flight, and I don't like to fly. Have you ever been, Thomas? You must still have family over there?"

"I think there is but I wouldn't know them. I've never had any contact with them and I don't think my father or mother stayed in touch with any family when they moved here."

"What did your parents do for work?" Mack inquired.

"After they'd arrived, my father was offered a good position with a law firm in Portland. The firm paid well and, in 1927, they moved here. They rented this cottage first, and then bought it a few years later. My mother never worked, even during the Depression, and enjoyed visiting friends and drinking tea. My father worked all the time. He had one bad temper. He used to scare the crap out of me."

They took a sip of their drinks.

"Were you their only child?" Mack asked, completely fascinated.

Thomas appeared lost in thought. "No. I had an older brother, Charlie. He died toward the end of the Second World War, and a sister...she died a few years later. My mother died of a heart condition in 1951, and my father in 1964. I hadn't spoken to my father for years when he died, so I was surprised that he'd left everything to me. That's when I changed the name of the cottage." He sighed heavily, and Mack could tell that he'd had enough for one night.

"Thank you for telling me about your family. You have a very good memory for dates."

"I've always been good with figures," he replied. "I think I'll call it a night."

Mack watched Thomas and as he got to his feet, she asked, "Please join us for breakfast."

His weathered face creased into a delighted smile. "I have breakfast plans, but I will call in on my way home." Without another word he left and the silence was only broken when Lucas charged into the kitchen.

"I heard you invite Mr. Degan for breakfast, do you think I could sleep on the sofa tonight and wait for him to come back?"

With a soft laugh, Mack ushered him upstairs. "I think you'll be up well before he arrives after breakfast so there is no need to sleep on the sofa." In the bathroom she started to run his bath while she silently smiled at her nephew who currently leaned against the doorjamb.

He moaned and groaned and muttered to himself under the impression that his auntie had no idea what he was saying. She heard everyone of his complaints about how grown ups were bossy.

Schooling her features she turned and grinned. "If you want to see Mr. Degan in the morning then I suggest you run and get your pajamas. We'll put them on the heater so that they're nice and warm for when you get out of the bath." Her words ended up lost because Lucas had already run like a bullet to his room.

Hopefully he'd sleep after the fresh air of the coast.

CHAPTER TWO

"Auntie Mack, Auntie Mack, it's time to get up." Lucas shouted, running into Mack's bedroom, seconds before diving onto the bed. "Come on, Auntie. You have to wake up. The birds told me it's time for breakfast." He paused for a breath. "They want pancakes and ketchup."

Mack slowly opened her eyes and moved the quilt away from her face. She took one look at her very excited nephew and slowly registered hearing pancakes and ketchup in the same sentence.

"Lucas, you don't eat pancakes and ketchup together. That's, well...not done." She glanced toward the clock on the side table and rubbed her eyes. She really needed glasses because she was sure the clock read not much past five. She rubbed her eyes again. "Oh my,

Lucas, it's only ten past five in the morning. Nobody gets up at this time." She dropped her head back to the pillow, took hold of Lucas, and helped get him under the covers with her. "Now, go back to sleep… *Please?*"

"What time can I get up?" Lucas asked, already half-asleep.

"I'll wake you up in a couple of hours." She turned her head to look at him, only to find that he was already fast asleep.

"Are you really, really, sure I can't have ketchup with my pancakes?" Lucas whined, looking sullen.

"Lucas, you do not put ketchup on pancakes. It was made to go on fries, which is why they made syrup to go on pancakes."

While she had a glaring match with him, Mack placed the syrup on the table beside his plate, along with a glass of chocolate milk.

"Wow, chocolate milk," he exclaimed. "Syrup is good."

She turned away so Lucas wouldn't see the amusement on her face.

Taking her seat, she started to wake up as the first sip of delicious coffee trickled down her throat.

After breakfast, she followed Lucas into the living room and switched the Wii on for him to play for a short while. "Don't have it on too loud, okay?"

"I won't." He grinned.

Mack left him to it while she wandered over to the bookshelf on the far wall in the living room. She took one of the old hardbacks out and had to blow the dust away in order to read the title, 'Gone with the Wind.' Her eyes widened at finding such a treasure and they widened even more when she realized that she held a first edition in her hands.

"Why would such a book be left in a summer rental?" she mumbled to herself while stroking the old bound cover. As she slipped it back into its slot on the shelf, she wondered what other treasures lay covered with dust, but before she could look, there was a brief knock on the door. Before she could answer Thomas walked in. "Morning, Miss Mackenzie. Hope you had a good night's rest."

"I did, thank you." She'd just finished speaking as Lucas ran in from the living room, straight to Thomas, who bent down and gave him a big hug.

"I was wondering if I could take the boy for a couple of hours?" Thomas asked, pulling a chair out at the table before taking the weight off his legs.

Mack needed a few minutes to think because although she felt like she'd known Thomas a long time, she didn't really know him... Lucas certainly wouldn't have a problem going with him, so while she thought about his request, she asked, "Would you like coffee?"

He nodded, removing his cap.

Mack poured a cup for them both and joined him at the table. "Do you know that you have a first edition of Gone with the Wind on the bookshelf in the living room?"

Thomas smiled softly. "It belonged to my mother, but it was my sisters favorite book.

That's why it's still there." He shrugged. "About borrowing Lucas…"

Mack smiled. "What do you have planned today?"

"I was thinking that I have a lot of those comics, like we were reading yesterday, in a box in the garage. I thought maybe Lucas could help bring them into the house so we can take a look through them together."

"What a lovely idea. Thank you for asking him, Thomas. By the look of things, Lucas would love that."

"I'll go wash up again. Be back in a minute." Lucas bounded upstairs to the bathroom.

She burst out laughing due to Lucas's rather exuberant reaction, and watched him retreat. Turning back to Thomas, she said, "Thank you for telling me about your family last night. I really enjoyed listening. I hope you didn't think that I was being nosy."

"I haven't really spoken about them for a very long time, and I quite enjoyed sitting here, drinking coffee while I talked about them with you."

"I'm glad. I was slightly worried after

you left, in case talking about them had upset you."

He shook his head. "It was a long time ago. I was fine."

Mack nodded. "Are you sure you don't mind having Lucas? He can be a handful." Mack frowned. She was a lot younger than Thomas was, and Lucas could probably tire a lion out with the amount of energy he seemed to have. Heaven knew the number of times he'd tired her out.

"Don't worry yourself. If there's a problem, I have your cell number, and I only live five minutes down the footpath."

On his reappearance, Lucas slipped his hand inside Thomas's much larger one.

"Bye, Auntie Mack."

Mack smiled. "Bye, Lucas. You behave yourself if you want any chance of being invited back."

Lucas grinned. "I will."

"See you, Thomas. And thank you again." She watched them walk off down the footpath hand in hand.

~

"Mr. Degan," Lucas asked. "How old are these comics? There's a lot of dust." He sneezed.

Thomas laughed and coughed at the same time. "I've had these since I was a youngster. I started buying them with my allowance in 1942 and bought them for about five years, I think." He frowned. "Why don't you call me Thomas?"

Lucas grinned, and repeated, "Thomas."

"That's it." Thomas smiled at the delight on the boys young face.

"Can I have a look inside this one, please?" Lucas asked, waving a rather grue-some covered comic in the air.

"That's a Halloween edition. Take a seat, and I'll bring you some milk and cookies."

"Yummy." Then he remembered his manners. "Thank you."

Thomas headed into the kitchen, trying to remember the last time he'd had so much fun. Sadly, he couldn't. His wife, Janet, had died when they were both fifty-six. That was twenty-four years ago. They hadn't been blessed with children of their own. Janet had been an only child, and both of

Thomas's siblings had died years before, so he had no nieces or nephews, just children of friends, who he'd become an honorary uncle to over the years.

It had really been too long since a child had visited inside his house.

Mack hadn't realized how many of her books she'd actually brought with her until she'd unpacked them into neat piles on the top shelf of the closet, in the hope that Lucas wouldn't be able to reach them.

With the boxes dismantled, she dragged a chair over to the kitchen counter, and climbing up, hoped there were no spiders as she carefully placed the flattened boxes on top. A thump and the boxes not sliding into place stopped her with a frown. She lifted the boxes and peered beneath, only to find what looked to be a book of some sort, covered in a thick layer of dust. She reached for the book, and then quickly laid the boxes down before she jumped back to the floor.

Grabbing a cloth, Mack wiped the thick covering of dust from the cover.

Due to her love of all things historic, her skin tingled as she held the long forgotten tome. It looked really old and must have been up there a long time. Mack stroked the front of the soft, leather-bound, book before peeling it open to the first page . . .

This is the diary of a Rose
March 4, 1947

"Oh, my." Mack lowered herself onto a kitchen chair. Stunned. The diary was...seventy years old, and who was Rose? Why was her diary on top of the kitchen cabinets? Mack could hardly contain her curiosity.

"Auntie Mack, I'm home!" Lucas ran into the kitchen.

Her heart raced with excitement at the discovery of the diary. She certainly didn't want Lucas getting wind of what she had. He'd be searching high and low for it, so he could read it himself.

Thomas followed behind Lucas, and glancing at Mack, frowned. But when he noticed what she held in her hands, he lost all color.

Mack watched him carefully, and asked, "Do you know anything about this book, Thomas? It says *this is the diary of a Rose,'* and it's dated 1947...a relative?" Mack waited for his response and realized that Thomas was perhaps in shock. "Thomas, are you feeling all right?" She moved closer.

"Yes, yes, fine. I need to get home." He started to move toward the door.

"But isn't this yours? After all, it's your family's cottage."

Thomas turned back around to look at her. "It's okay, you found it so read it first, and then pass it on to me. Have a good evening."

Then he was gone, just like that.

That evening, Mack checked on Lucas to make sure he was asleep, before she headed downstairs to make a steaming cup of hot chocolate. She'd already showered and changed into her pajamas, but her mind wasn't ready for sleep yet.

As she stirred the hot milky drink, she

couldn't stop thinking about the diary that she'd discovered earlier in the day. Someone's life was between those pages and she felt excitement at the discovery. She frowned though as she remembered Thomas's reaction to the name Rose. What had that been about?

Her thoughts slipped from her mind as she sipped the hot chocolate, and headed upstairs to the bedroom. She kept her door slightly ajar to listen for Lucas as she settled into bed. Then she picked up the diary and turned it to the first page.

CHAPTER THREE

This is the diary of a Rose . . .

March 4, 1947

My name is Rose Degan and I am 19 years old.

This is my first diary.

After the events of yesterday, I have decided I must keep one.

Yesterday was a very exciting day in Cape Elizabeth, and in my life, because I met the most handsome man . . .

I worked in the town library, and today I was in the history section dusting the shelves and the books. It really was the worst job Mr. Young, my boss, could give anyone, and for some reason he seemed to like giving it to me.

At the nine mark, my brother JT nearly knocked me off my ladder as he came running around the corner. He was so out of breath that I started to panic. "JT, what is it? Is everyone all right?" I asked, franticly searching him up and down for any injuries.

"Sis, will you take me to watch the rescue at sea?"

"What are you talking about?" JT had been known to spin a yarn now and again.

"Walt said a collier ship has gone

aground at Two Lights because of the storm. Please, will you take me?"

I could tell Mr. Young a little white lie, it wasn't as though I was busy, and the dust would still be there tomorrow. That decided, I took JT by the hand and briefly left him with Emma while I went in search of Mr. Young to tell him I was sick with a 'female' problem.

Not long after, I walked out of his office, grinning. My boss had reacted as I thought he would. First, he'd turned bright red like a tomato and then he'd plopped down in his chair. He probably hoped I wasn't about to divulge further details.

Quickly grabbing my things and JT, we walked toward the wreckage, along with a lot of townsfolk.

As we approached, we could hear everyone cheering. It sounded more like a party rather than a rescue.

Sarah, a friend from school, was standing not too far away with her older sister. As soon as she spotted us, we started to walk over to them, which was getting rather difficult with JT trying to pull me in a different direction.

"Sis, I want to go over there to Walt and Levi," JT said, tugging on my hand for the umpteenth time.

"Let me go and talk to Sarah first to find out what's going on. Then I'll take you over there."

I ignored JT while he groaned and grumbled about why he always had to do what the grown-ups told him to do.

"Sarah, what's happening here?" I asked after we finished hugging. Sarah was the friendliest of people and always 'hugged.' She used to make me feel uncomfortable but, after a while, I enjoyed the familiarity.

"They shot a breeches buoy to the vessel and now they're rescuing crew members. Whenever they bring another to shore safely, everyone cheers."

"I wonder if they need help with any-thing," I said, only to have Sarah's sister scowl at me. Miss Prim-and-Proper Matilda.

Finally, after about ten minutes of making polite conversation, I allowed JT to steer me toward Levi and Walt, his two best friends and, on more than one occasion, partners in crime.

There was still a bit of a chill in the air and gusts of wind kept wrapping around me, moving me around while I tried to keep an eye on JT. There was enough commotion without JT and his friends causing any more trouble.

Glancing around, I noticed a really handsome man with his eyes on me. I froze, and in that moment, all sound ceased to exist, and we were the only ones there. Unfortunately, I soon came back to my senses when he started to walk toward me with a nonchalant grace, causing my heart to flutter wildly in my chest.

He was tall, beardless, with an ingenuously appealing face. His massive shoulders filled the coat he wore and his stance emphasized the force of his thighs and the slimness of his hips. A swath of dark brown wavy hair fell casually on his forehead, giving him a boyish charm.

His lips twitched as he stood in front of me, his eyes holding mine, filled with amusement. "Hello," he said, his voice chocolate smooth. "I haven't seen you around before." He smiled, his teeth strikingly white against his tanned face.

"I'm Rose." I nervously held my handout to him in greeting, and the minute our palms connected, I felt as though I'd been struck by lightning. If the surprise on his face was anything to go by, he'd felt it too.

He cleared his throat. "Jacob Evans. I've been in Cape Elizabeth about a month now. Do you live around here?" His eyes held mine.

"Not too far away, near the beach. I work in town at the library."

My hand was still clenched tightly in his when JT came running over. "Sis?" He looked back and forth between the two of us. "What's going on? Why are you talking to him?" he asked, pointing at Jacob. "You're supposed to be marrying Richard, you can't talk to him."

I blushed at JT's impetuous remark. He was a teenager, and I really wished I could shut him up, especially since he'd mentioned Richard. Ugh. *Brothers!*

I quickly glanced at Jacob for his reaction to my brothers words and disappointment crossed his features before he released my hand and stepped back.

"Rose, come on," JT said, whose impatience was really starting to irritate me.

"I better go with him. I hope to see you again," I said, as JT finally succeeded in dragging me away.

"I hope so," he said with a trace of yearning in his voice.

Before I lost sight of him completely, I glanced back, only to find his eyes locked on my retreating figure. My heart had yet to stop its rapid beating. Such a feeling was entirely new to me.

"Sis, you shouldn't be talking to strange men when you're marrying Richard."

"JT, I am not marrying Richard, not now, not ever, and one day Mother and Father will realize that."

After dinner, my best friend Jayne called at the house. I dragged her around the side to sit in the garden. I didn't want anyone overhearing what I had to tell her but, by the end of the evening, I wish I'd kept it to myself, as she told me I was being stupid. That no one could be infatuated with someone they had only just met.

March 8, 1947

Richard came calling today . . .

It had been four days since I'd seen Jacob, and every time I walked through town, I found myself looking for him. Why hadn't I asked him where he worked? I told him I worked at the library but, perhaps, he didn't want to see me, which distressed me more than it ought.

While I'd been spending my time dreaming about Jacob, my mother had been filling my mind with all things Richard. Richard was the only child of Bernard and Evelyn, who so happened to own the local newspaper, a hotel in Boston, and a few other local businesses. So, of course, he was a great catch. Mother didn't seem to understand that I wanted to marry for love, not money.

Richard was a really good-looking man —tall, blond hair with blue eyes, but he had more interest in tinkering with cars than he did in me, or anyone else for that matter. I actually found him boring. On both of the two dates I'd been on with him, I couldn't wait to get back home. I'd only agreed to go on them to stop my parents from bothering me about him.

Today, I was lying in the hammock in the garden in an attempt to hide. Mother had allergies for about everything you could get an allergy for, so despite her love of the garden, she never actually went into it. She certainly wouldn't risk getting all blotchy to find me. At least, I hoped she wouldn't.

"Rose, you in here?"

"Richard?" He nearly had me falling out of the hammock. "What are you doing here?"

"I've come to see you, isn't it obvious?"

Why did that reply make me feel nervous?

He helped me out of the hammock and led me over to the bench inside the newly built gazebo.

"How have you been, Rose?" He shuffled his feet, gazing nervously around the garden.

"I'm fine. Thank you for asking. How are you?" I really hated polite conversation.

"Good, good." He started to pace back and forth in front of me.

"Richard... Please stop. You're making me dizzy," I said as I watched him. "Whatever is the matter?"

He stopped pacing and said the one word I didn't want to hear. "Marriage."

When I heard it, I shot up off the bench and stood in front of him. "Please do not ask me to marry you. We don't even know each other," I begged.

"It's what our parents want." He moved away from me and sank to the bench before he looked out at the sea, deep in thought.

"Richard, do you love me?" I stood to the side of him, awaiting his reply.

He looked at me. "No."

I sighed in relief. "I don't love you either, and when I marry, it will be for love, and not because of our parents. That's what you should want as well. How do you expect to be happy if you're not in love with your wife?"

He took my hand and pulled me down beside him onto the bench. "Oh, Rose, thank you for being so frank with me. I agree with you. I'm not interested in settling down into marriage yet. In fact, perhaps it's time I start leading my own life, rather than being dictated to all the time. I would dearly value your friendship, though."

I smiled up at him. "Friendship would be lovely," I agreed in relief.

Now available from all online retailers.

ACKNOWLEDGMENTS

Editors: Abigail Higson and Sirena van Schaik

Cover Designer: Robin Harper, Wicked by Design

BETA Readers: Emma Clifton, Jo Magson, Kathrin Magyar, Laura Ward, Nadine Winningham, Sonya Covert, and Lynne Garlick

To my family who had to search through washing baskets for clean clothes, had 'something quick' for dinner, lived in an upside down house, while I concentrated on this book, I love you all.

Kathrin, thank you for your friendship, for organizing me (which isn't easy), and for being my overseas travel partner—I love and appreciate you so much!

Lynne & Cara, thank you both for your friendship. Lynne, you read every word I write, even the brief chapters for books that won't get completed for years—thank you!

OTHER BOOKS BY AUTHOR

Bad Boy Rockers

Book 1: My Brother's Girl (Sizzle) (Jack 'Jack' & Thalia)

Book 2: Past Sins (Spicy) (Reece & Callie)

Book 3: My Best Friend's Sister (Sultry) (Donovan & Mara)

Book 4: Never Let Go (Savor) (Ryder & Dahlia)

Book 5: Saving Jace (Sinful) (Jace & Savannah)

Book 6: Silent Night (Novella)

Kincaid Sisters

Book 1: Meant to be Mine

Book 2: You Were Always Mine (coming soon)

Book 3: Will You be Mine (coming soon)

McKenzie Brothers

Book 1: Seduce (Michael & Lily)

Book 1.5: The Wedding (Novella)

Book 2: Rapture (Sebastian & Carla)

Book 3: Delight (Ruben & Rosie)

Book 4: Entice (Lucien & Sabrina)

Book 5: Cherished (Ramon & Noah)

Book 5.5: A McKenzie Christmas (Novella)

De La Fuente Family (McKenzie Spinoff)

Book 1: Love in Montana (Sylvia & Eric)

Book 2: Love in Purgatory (Dante & Emelia)

Book 3: Love in Bloom (Mateo & Erin)

Book 4: Love in Country (Aiden & Sarah)

Book 5: Love in Flame (Diego & Rae)

Book 6: Love in Game (Kasey & Felicity)

Book 7: Love in Education (Andie & Seth)

McKenzie Cousins
(McKenzie Spinoff)

Book 1: Baby Makes Three (Sirena & Garrett)

Book 2: A Business Decision (Michael & Brooke)

Book 3: Secret Kisses (Charlotte & Tanner)

Book 4: Kissing Cousins (Rachel & Alexander)

Book 5: If Only (Madison & Derek)

Book 6: Princess & the Puck (Paige & Seth)

Book 7: A Bakers Delight (Sofia & Shane)

Book 8: A Cowboy for Christmas (Olivia & Geary)

Book 9: A Secret Affair (Joshua & Mallory)

Book 10: One Christmas (Dylan & Jenna)

Book 11: The Pregnant Professor (Jaxon & Poppy)

Book 12: It Started with a Kiss (Ryan & Gretchen)

Jackson Hole

Book 1: From This Moment

Book 1.5: When we Meet (Novella, in the back of From This Moment)

Book 2: New Beginning (coming soon)

Romantic Suspense

Lawful

Stryker

Standalone Novella's

One Dance

Educate Me

Pure

Holiday Season

Kissing Under the Mistletoe

A Soldier's Christmas

Jingle Bells

Written as Rona Jameson

Butterfly Girl

Come Back to Me

Summer at Rose Cottage

Tears in the Rain

Twenty Eight Days

ABOUT THE AUTHOR

English born Rona Jameson is an author of romance who currently resides in Ireland with her husband, four children, one dog, three cats, and a guinea pig named Merry. She's been writing since 2013 as Lexi Buchanan, which is where you can find her more explicit writing.

Follow on social media:

Website: http://ronajameson.com
Email: authorlexibuchanan@gmail.com

f facebook.com/lexibuchananauthor
🐦 twitter.com/AuthorLexi
📷 instagram.com/authorlexib
BB bookbub.com/author/lexi-buchanan

Printed in Poland
by Amazon Fulfillment
Poland Sp. z o.o., Wrocław

55012689R00233